IDYLLIC AVENUE

CHAD GANSKE

03.15.2018

www.crescentmoonpress.com

Idyllic Avenue
Chad Ganske

ISBN: 978-1-939173-70-6
E-ISBN: 978-1-939173-71-3

Editor: Sheldon Reid
Layout/Typesetting: jimandzetta.com

Crescent Moon Press
1385 Highway 35
Box 269
Middletown, NJ 07748

Crescent Moon Press electronic publication/print publication: February 2014 www.crescentmoonpress.com

"It is interesting to contemplate a tangled bank, clothed with many plants of many kinds, with birds singing on the bushes, with various insects flitting about, and with worms crawling through the damp earth..."

--Charles Darwin

For my couplet... forever in dreams

0.5 (PROLOGUE)

The bombings were into their third week, with no sign of relenting. Brilliant fires of crimson and ash rose up from the industrialized sector as the Militia engaged with the Tech Terrorists for control of the quadrants. The insurgents aimed to cut off the flow of supplies into the elite colony, punishing the Patron's favorite children. A rebel stronghold in the mutant colony would give the terrorists control of the largest population on the planet *Ultim*. Once they had the mutants, the smaller colony of elitists would fall to its knees in a matter of days.

The rebels were a select group of solitaries – mutants who had once lived alone in the large colony. Tired of waiting for mandatory coupling, they banded together to protest their exclusion from the *Salus* dome with extreme force. The Militia had repelled their initial attack thirty years earlier, irradiating the insurgent camps with nuclear weapons and banishing their kind to the outer boundaries. The rebel cell was thought to have perished under the effects of the radiation, with the few survivors doomed to live out their days hiding amongst the ash dunes.

Now they had returned – fewer in numbers but armed with survival instincts fiercer than ever. They were keenly aware that Ultim was the final landing ground for the human species. Evacuation shuttles had long become inoperable, and there was nowhere to go otherwise. With no other choice but death, the Tech Terrorists refused to be omitted from the immaculate

~ ☾ ~

new society under the protective dome when the binary suns turned to pulsars. They fought bitterly for their inclusion by any means necessary.

The Patron was protected by his Militia, and as long as he was in power, the only way for a mutant to gain entrance to Salus was by serving the Policy.

"To those mutants who have successfully served the Policy, take heart, for you will be granted entrance into the artificial environment when the suns extinguish. Once inside Salus you will be sheltered by an atmospheric dome specifically designed for our long-term survival. Our dome is strong enough to protect us from external forces, both natural and unnatural, and sensitive enough to predict even the slightest variations in our skies.

"Our meteorologists pay strict attention to air composition and quality. In the case of undesirable changes in atmospheric conditions, the dome is designed to expel toxins through its membrane until the desired state is achieved once again. It is in a continuous state of regulation.

"Inside Salus, you will have access to all the environment has to offer. Fresh produce and meat will be shipped to stores in your community on a daily basis, originating from the very same farms and orchards enjoyed by the general population. Clean drinking water will be provided via streams that run directly through the heart of your sector. You will have access to hunting grounds where you can seek out wild game and enjoy dinner killed with your very own hands. Fishing reservoirs will be in abundance. You and your couplet can live with more amenities than you ever had access to in the past.

"Consider the artificial environment a place where you will live an enhanced version of the life you have previously known, with more security and freedom than you have ever experienced. Feel free to interact

~ ☾ ~

with all of your fellow colonists without trepidation, for our society has been cleansed of all known sickness and genetic disorders to ensure our longevity as a strong and healthy race. And, if you have the fortune of meeting with your offspring, you can share the splendor of all that Salus has to offer a family reunited.

"Please accept this gift for successfully serving the Policy. Life doesn't end after the suns extinguish – it only gets better."

~ ☾ ~

PART I: (THE POLICY)

1.0

Stanford watched the flecks of copper shimmering within his irises in the reflection of the en suite mirror. The fragments were the size of pinpricks, orbiting his pupils like planetary rings. They always shone brightest in the morning. In thirty-six years staring at his reflection, he had never gotten used to the strange genetic anomaly.

Self-conscious, he pivoted away from the mirror and stripped out of his robe to enter the condensation booth. Inside, the chamber filled with a dense cloud of steam that settled on his skin and collected the grime from his pores. It felt good in the booth, warm, and he sat on the meditation cushion, allowing the cloud to envelope him like a womb. The moisture filled his lungs, relaxing his body, and just as the booth began to pull him into sleep, the whir of the intake fan pulled him back.

When he stepped out, the dog met him on the bath mat and eagerly licked the traces of water from the tops of his feet. It was good to see the old collie behaving naturally. He would need to keep a close eye on the dog to make sure there were no abnormalities after the reversal. A second procedure was risky, he'd been told, but it was better than seeing the old boy struggle around on arthritic hips.

Watching the collie poke curiously through the bathroom now, he seemed as good as new, maybe better than before. There was even a hint of playfulness as he followed the old boy through the doorway into the adjoining bedroom.

~ ☾ ~

Stanford walked under the intense arc of light that beamed from the transmitter on the nightstand; he examined the dial on the little black box before pressing the *off* button. The room went instantly black, and he could see a figure watching from the doorway.

A slight wave of irritation hit him when his wife flipped on the EM tubes to reintroduce light in the bedroom. She had primped herself before completion of the sleep cycle, taking great effort to bundle her voluminous brown hair elaborately atop her head, coordinating brown flats with a beige knee-length skirt and a pressed eggshell blouse. He was irritated by how well she was put together, and even more so by how rested she appeared.

She seemed to sense his discomfort.

"How did you sleep?" she asked.

He could barely stand the sight of her pristine image. "Isn't it obvious?"

"Was there a problem with the arc?"

"You have to ask? It was too high. My melatonin is completely out of balance."

"Maybe you should have it checked. It's been a while since we had somebody in to measure the levels."

"How can you be unaffected?"

"You know I don't need the arc to sleep. Maybe you've become reliant."

"Did you adjust the setting?"

She looked at him coldly. "Why would I do that? You should try counting sheep," she snapped.

He turned away from her frosty glare and looked blankly into the closet. "I'm sorry," he said. "You know how I get when I don't complete my cycle."

She approached from behind, laying a hand on his shoulder and massaging his tense neck. "I know," she said. "Let me help you." She pushed gently by and located the overalls with ease. The task was much less burdensome for her rested mind.

~ ☾ ~

He watched her lay the overalls on the bed and smooth out the wrinkles with her hand. She did everything with grace.

"Did you dream?" she asked.

He looked at her curiously. "Why do you want to know?"

"I want to know what you dreamed about."

"My dreams are my own, Sarah. If I tell you, it could cross-contaminate the transmission. You know how it works as well as I do."

She tried to coerce him with her overemphasized pout. "Won't you just tell me a bit? There's no harm in sharing small details."

"If you slept under the arc you would have dreams of your own and you wouldn't have to steal mine."

"Come on, Stanford."

"Sarah, please."

"Where were you? At least tell me that much."

Stanford hesitated before finally relenting. She had a way of pursing her lips in a mock sulk he couldn't resist.

"I was here – in this house. I was watching the war through the living room window."

"You're not old enough to remember the war, Stanford."

"I remember some ... I thought you wanted to know."

"I do. I'm sorry. Were you alone?"

"You were with me. That's all I'm saying."

"Was it just us?"

"Please, Sarah." Stanford knew exactly what she was fishing for but was reluctant to give in. He wanted her to remain realistic about their life together, not live in the constructs of his subconscious.

She was unremitting, however. Her prior attempts at seductive coercion turned to shameless groveling. "That's all I want to know," she begged. "I won't ask anything else."

He couldn't take it anymore. His head pounded.

~ ☾ ~

"There was a child," he huffed. There was no point in hiding it. She had suspected it all along.

She stepped towards him. "Was it ours?"

He felt uncomfortable with her closeness. Her dominant brown eyes seemed to look right through him. "That's all I'm saying."

"Was it eradicated?"

"I don't know. It was a dream."

"Please, Stanford, tell me!"

"Yes, Sarah, it was eradicated. Are you happy now?"

Her pout turned into a victorious smile, and she wrapped her arms around his neck. "Thank you. I don't mind if your dream crosses into me," she said. "That sounds so wonderful."

"Don't count on it. The transmission is stifled." He felt a moment of guilt for trying to smother her optimism, but it passed quickly.

There was a momentary pause in her enthusiasm; just a slight flinch. "Come have breakfast," she said. "It will help you feel better." She stopped when she reached the doorway. "Stanford?"

"Yes?"

"Thank you for sharing."

He stared at the empty doorframe after she was gone and struggled to pull his shirt over his head. Even putting on his socks was a chore. He could feel stray bits of energy surging in his temples as a result of the faulty transmitter. A failed signal stirred the brain chemistry in such a way that it often caused a sensation similar to a hangover. He knew it would take time for his mind to settle.

As he slipped into his overalls he wondered why she pressed so hard for details. Perhaps she hadn't been dreaming at all and purposely hoped for cross-contamination in order to spark her own imagination. Maybe she preferred his dreams to her own, especially since his mind seemed intent on a recurring baby theme. There was no sense in dwelling on it. He had

~ ☾ ~

spent far too much time on it already. The child would come when the conditions were right and not before. He shook his head to loosen the jumbled thoughts and stared down at the collie sleeping between the legs of the dormant robot aide tucked away in the far corner. It was the most production he had seen out of the aide for several days.

At least it's good for something, he thought, *even if it's just a pillow for the dog.*

He made his way down the hallway towards the kitchen, temples throbbing, and could hear the Patron's voice filtering through the radio.

"Permanent midnight is on the horizon. We must view the extinguishing of the twin suns not as an end, but as a chance for a new beginning — an opportunity to cleanse our collective skin and start anew. The way to salvation is through the self-sustained bio-dome, free of the ills that have nipped at the heels of mankind throughout history. The artificial environment inside Salus will offer all that we consider good – fresh water, fertile land, minerals for mining – without the disease and rot that has plagued us until now.

"The new society will exist not in sickness but in health ..."

Stanford watched his wife from the archway as she worked about the kitchen. Her hips were perfect for childbearing, wider than her shoulders, though not disproportionate. The apron's drawstrings fastened around an hourglass waist. She was slight in stature, vulnerable, but a strong woman in so many ways. He felt a moment of contentedness as he moved to switch off the radio before approaching the table.

Sitting, he heard her say, "You know I like to listen while I cook."

He looked towards her. "I don't know why you get your hopes up about Salus. We're stuck here."

"Stuck? Is that what you call it?"

~ ☾ ~

He could tell she was different now. The grace she had shown earlier had been replaced by movements that were more deliberate; she refused to look at him. When she placed the serving dish on the centerpiece he leaned forward for a better look at the offering.

"Are these genuine?" he asked, referring to the sunny side eggs.

Her eyes were pointed at him but did not take him in. "The vendor told me they were imported from the artificial environment," she said matter-of-factly.

"These are from Salus?"

She looked away. "Two are for you."

Stanford took his time selecting two hearty eggs and waited while she sat down opposite of him. He imagined the bright yolks were the faces of the twin suns erupting like blinding flares on the horizon. He was almost trance-like when he pierced the yellow membranes with his fork and watched the viscous fluid drift across the plate. When he glanced back at his wife he couldn't help but feel contrite. She did so much to please him. His unstable mind made it difficult to contain his outbursts; he knew exactly what hurt her the most. He should not have told her about the dream, nor should he have spoiled her enthusiasm towards Salus. He reached across to gently touch her hand.

"I'll stop off at the Robot Emporium on my way to work," he said. "There will be discounts on the old stock."

Now she acknowledged him. "I like to cook for you."

"I know," he said. "I just want to get you some help. I don't think there's any point putting more money into the old aide. We're throwing good money after bad."

He watched a smile etch across her face. She was coming back to life.

"I forgot the coffee," she said.

She suddenly seemed reinvigorated as she went to fetch the thermos.

Stanford felt better that she felt better. "Did the

~ ☾ ~

vendor say anything more about the environment?" he asked while she was up.

"Not much. Just that it will start producing more and more as it gets up and running. Eggs, chicken, beef. Everything we had before. There's so much to look forward to."

She poured the steaming coffee into his mug and retook her seat.

As he shoveled in another bite he saw the dog wander casually in and sniff around at spots on the floor.

"Stanford?"

He looked back at his wife. "Yes?"

"Can I ride the train with you?"

"Of course you can."

"Audrey has been pestering me to go shopping."

"That will be good for you." He paused a moment, deliberating. "I meant to ask you if you dreamed last night. I figured it was okay to ask since you asked first."

She smiled as she stood up to gather the plates. She was so beautiful. If they truly were stuck, he was happy to be stuck with her. He was glad for their arrangement.

She looked over her shoulder as she loaded the sanitizing machine. "I don't rely on the arc, Stanford, but that doesn't mean I don't dream."

"So tell me."

She laughed. "My dreams belong to me, you said so yourself!"

Out of the corner of his eye, Stanford saw the dog lift its hind leg and urinate on a spot near the entranceway, whimper, and slink out on his belly.

Sarah's mood shifted at once. "Oh ... Stanford ..."

Her brown eyes grew plaintive.

"We should not have gone ahead with the second reversal," she said. "His poor body ..."

Stanford felt the negative energy surging through his temples again.

Poor old boy ...

~ ☾ ~

2.0 (SARAH)

Sarah Samuels gripped her husband's hand as the atoms crackled in the engine and propelled the fusion train like a dart along the downtown line.

When the train accelerated, the hydrogen emitted enough energy to rattle the undersides of the passenger seats, lifting the carts an inch or so off the tracks to eliminate friction. Then it glided smoothly along a trajectory maintained by the magnetic bond with the rail. The liftoff was exhilarating, and when the train reached cruising speed, Sarah resisted the urge to squeeze her husband's hand. The popping sound of atoms fusing together reminded her of exploding popcorn kernels.

As the train whisked through the boundary of the residential sector, she watched her husband sleeping next to her in the double clamshell and felt a tightening in her chest. It was during moments of peace that she felt the weight of her burden. Like the other Eradicators living in the mutant colony, Sarah had been brought here under the mandate of the Cleansing Policy, a biological experiment designed to boost the healthy population of "Perfects" before the suns burned out. Eradicators were former residents of the Perfect colony, strategically selected to be *coupled* with mutants based on the probability of their chromosomes wiping out the mutant gene in any potential offspring. The reward for offering a genetically cleansed child to the healthy colony was safe passage to Salus for both eradicating parents. This offering was called "Serving the Policy." The mission of the Eradicators was critical to the long-

~ ☾ ~

term survival of the human race, as the Perfect colony served as the feeding tube to Salus.

Sarah glanced at her husband. With his eyes closed, there was not a hint of his mutation. It was like that for many of the mutants. A flawed gene could reveal itself in numerous forms. An alcoholic was a mutant, as was a cancer patient, a blind man, a deaf woman. Sarah's genetics alone were responsible for eradicating Stanford's flaw. Failing the project would result in their exclusion from Salus. With great responsibility came grave consequences for Eradicators and their mutant couplets.

Thinking about it gave her the sudden urge to kiss her husband and apologize for the trouble he had experienced all morning, but she didn't dare. It would likely be the only moment he had for peace. Instead, she sought distraction by turning her attention out the window at the blur of small shrubs and sparse patches of wild grass that somehow sprouted in the contaminated soil. An entire new generation had grown up on this desolate landscape, never having witnessed the fertility that existed before the nuclear war. Sarah felt a fleeting wave of hope that the plants of her youth would flourish again, but soon the vegetation was replaced by a concrete slab as the fusion train entered the hub of the mutant colony.

Right on cue, the familiar message came through the loudspeakers in the terminal.

"Have you served the Policy today? If you haven't updated your coupling profile with Central Registration, please stop at any one of our government kiosks in the terminal to do so. Updating your code is critical to ensuring the accuracy of your match. Don't be left out in the cold. The suns are nearing their end. Your place in Salus depends on it ..."

Sarah brushed her hand lightly along the contour of her husband's jaw in an attempt to draw him gently out

~ ☾ ~

of sleep. When his eyelids parted, she could see the copper fragments were stationary in his irises, a sign his hormones were back in balance – that he was calm again.

"We're here," she whispered.

The look of disorientation began to melt from his features as he took in the familiar image of his wife. "How long was I out?"

"You slept the whole time. How do you feel?"

"I feel better."

She smiled and squeezed his hand. "I'm glad." His fleshy palm brought her comfort.

There was a little jolt now as the train settled back on the rail; green bulbs illuminated over the exits to announce the offloading. She prompted him to put on his double-tinted sunglasses.

Moving down the aisle through the section of single clamshells, she couldn't help but glance at the lonely solitaries who gathered their belongings from the overhead compartments. The waiting period for coupling had extended from months to years due to the influx of newly identified cases and the ongoing struggle to classify suitable Eradicators. The uncoupled mutants were forced to live with the fear that they might never be matched. Without a match, they would never get to Salus. Sarah felt a swell of anxiety as she pulled her husband quickly towards the exit.

Columns of steel and cement stood tall in the downtown core, breathing like living organisms. Old buildings were restored; new ones were erected next to the ruins of structures gutted by bombs three decades old. Past the pedestrian square, freeways twisted through interchanges and off-ramps so thick with hover vehicles that the highways themselves seemed fluid. The scene here was in stark contrast to the population crisis facing the Perfects beyond the walls.

On the platform were kiosks with mutants lined up in

~ ☾ ~

endless rows to update their profiles for coupling. Next to the kiosks were the donation stations, where eradicated children of five years old were offered to the healthy colony. The couplets stood together holding hands with their offspring until they reached the front of the line where the hand off took place. Once in the custody of the Militia, the child was led through the gate to the other side of the wall, entering into quarantine for examination by geneticists before being put up for adoption.

The transfer was formal and unspectacular. When the child was gone, the parents turned around and walked off as if it had been a simple exchange of goods and services. Contact with the offspring was cut off to mitigate the feelings of loss until their eventual reunion in Salus. Now salvation was ensured for both mutant and Eradicator, and the population in the Perfect colony increased by one; the Policy had been served.

Reaching the edge of the platform, Sarah looked high above the eighty-foot walls at the two burning globules that made their trek eastward along dual ecliptics. She shielded her eyes as she looked into the faces of the twin suns.

There was no way of pinpointing the exact date when the binary stars would shrink to pulsars, or even if their lifecycles were in perfect synchronicity. Regardless, a spectacular – if not catastrophic – event was imminent.

According to colonial scientists, the force of gas-expulsion from one exploding sun would most certainly extinguish its twin, leaving Ultim in a state of permanent midnight. It was a risk taken the moment the travelers had entered the volatile NGC 2770 galaxy and settled on the ground beneath the aging white dwarfs. Known for the destructive forces of the local star system, the galaxy was commonly referred to as the Supernova Factory. Despite the dangers, however, the passenger ships touched down on Ultim a century ago,

~ ☾ ~

their occupants having plundered their previous home planets in Omega Centauri, leaving a string of infertile and unlivable rocks floating uselessly in their wake. Each traveler knew full well that the odds of success on Ultim were stacked against them, but with no life-sustaining planets in the explored galaxies left to inhabit, there was no other choice.

For a time, Ultim was a perfect host. The habitation expanded, mining operations resumed, and a contingency plan was established to deal with the impending loss of the suns. Civilization was split into two incongruous colonies separated by walls to prevent cross-contamination. Exploration of the Supernova Factory for other potential habitations ceased and construction of the Salus bio-dome became the focus. Amidst the progress, the prospect of imminent danger remained at the forefront of the collective consciousness. The suns had grown exponentially hotter over the past few decades as they neared critical mass, and with each passing year, the Cleansing Policy became all the more urgent.

The only hope was in the shape of a dome called Salus.

The suns will be back tomorrow, Sarah thought, *but how many more tomorrows, I do not know.*

She kissed her husband and watched as he disappeared into the maw of commuters.

I love you, Stanford Samuels. Stay safe. Please think of me.

~ ☾ ~

2.5 (STANFORD)

The hover pods blew by at such a rate, Stanford could feel the air currents blasting his cheeks.

Prompted by the *WALK* signal, the crowd moved as a single entity across the street until the sound of an emergency siren came from high above. As pedestrians scattered to the safety of the curbs, the police pod descended from the sky and settled in the middle of the intersection. Firmly aground, the hatch doors opened and spit out two Militia men armed with assault rifles and a helix-sniffing canine. The dog was metal-plated, hind legs rippling with muscle and silvery sinew. Stanford was sure he could see genuine saliva dripping from the jaws of the mechanical beast.

The snarling animal was led on a leash towards the double doors of a tall, corner building and released inside.

Back at the pod cruiser, a megaphone atop the squad car provided an explanation.

"The situation will be dealt with swiftly and justly. Please remain where you are while the officers bring the operation to a conclusion. This is a military sting ordered by the Patron. Non-compliance will be viewed as a threat against the colony and will be dealt with accordingly. Thank you for your cooperation."

Before long, the officers reappeared at the front of the apartment complex, with two naked individuals in custody. The helix-sniffing dog nipped at the heels of the detainees as they were escorted back to the cruiser.

The megaphone recited the Miranda while the prisoners were deposited into the hatches.

~ ☾ ~

"In accordance with the statutes of the Patron's Cleansing Policy, you have been found in violation of criminal code 2343, which prohibits copulation outside an appointed coupling where potential replication and probable perpetuation of a mutant gene is likely. This offence is the most egregious under colonial law and is punishable to the full extent of the criminal code. Do you understand your rights as they have been explained to you?"

The mob cheered, taking great pleasure in the swift justice brought against the sexual deviants. The hatch doors were sealed and twin propulsion engines lifted the cruiser off the ground, leaving a trail of smoke in its wake.

Back on the street, the walk signal blinked and the crowd resumed the commute as if nothing had happened.

Why would two mutants take such a risk? Stanford wondered as he continued towards the Emporium. *Living as a solitary is certainly preferable to breaking the rules of the Policy. I'll never understand why these people aren't terrified of the helix-sniffing dogs. They're pure killing machines. What a way to go.*

I pity the two mutants, although the laws of the Policy are clearly stated. What makes them think they are above the laws of the Patron? Sex is not an act performed solely for pleasure, nor is it exclusively a symbol of union, but rather a process designed to cleanse the genetic pool for our future society. They would be better off waiting for their coupling like everybody else.

Stanford glanced at his watch and picked up his pace. He wanted to give himself time to browse the Emporium while still clocking in for the early shift at work. A deduction in pay would hinder his ability to purchase a new aide for Sarah.

~ ☾ ~

The giant box store was within sight, "*Robot Emporium*" blinking in pink neon. There was no way to miss it.

He began a brisk jog through the sea of commuters, suddenly feeling short on time.

~ ☾ ~

2.75 (ROBOT EMPORIUM)

The interior of the Emporium was so efficiently cooled it seemed to balance on the border between pleasantly crisp and uncomfortably frigid.

When he got through the revolving doors, Stanford stood motionless for a moment to gain his bearings. The air instantly chilled the sweat on his brow, causing him to shiver as he glanced around at hundreds of aisles of robot parts and accessories; he had no idea which way to walk first.

People milled in and out of aisles, through checkout stands with oversized boxes and carts piled precariously high with electronic arms and legs and skulls. Small children – those still too young for transfer to the Perfect colony, as well as those whom eradication had failed – produced an annoying white noise that filtered through the entire department store and created a buzz in his ear. Out the corner of his eye he could see a man in a blue apron approaching.

As soon as the man was within ten feet he greeted Stanford: "Hello, sir, what would you say if I told you I could pair you with the perfect robot aide today?"

"I'd say you're eager." Stanford shook the man's hand.

Cold flesh. Artificial circulatory system. This man is a robot, he thought. *It's common for androids to be placed in sales jobs these days.*

"I'm looking for an estimate on a new aide," said Stanford. "My wife's unit malfunctioned, and I want a sense of what's available. High efficiency is what she wants."

~ ☾ ~

"Of course," said the salesman. "Follow me. I'll show you where we keep the newest HE models."

The android moved quickly.

"I'm only browsing today," said Stanford, following close behind.

The salesman smiled over his shoulder. "Not a problem. I'll show you what we have in stock. I think you'll be duly impressed. Let's take a ride."

The android showed him to a golf cart. They climbed aboard the self-propelled vehicle and navigated down long aisles displaying metallic ankles and titanium thighs and buttocks. The cart turned several times and Stanford began to wonder how he would find his way back. He was sure there was a more direct route.

The cart stopped in a section where EM tubes shone down on an arrangement of brilliantly polished robots. Even through the tint of his glasses, he could see they were extraordinarily glossy.

"These are top of the line," said the android as he stepped out of the vehicle. "Each unit is preprogrammed with a brainstem chip. There's no post-purchase computer code to input, which saves the consumer programming costs down the line. Every unit accepts commands for laundry, kitchen duties, garbage disposal, vacuuming, bathrooms, you name it. There's nothing they can't do. Take a closer look."

Stanford got out of the cart and stepped towards the display case. The intelligent design impressed him. Each unit was positioned in such a way that its eyes seemed to follow wherever he went.

"Do they have internal cooling fans in the hard drive?" he asked.

"This model won't overheat, ever. Have you had problems with that in the past?"

"My old unit has a tendency to seize up."

"What model, if you don't mind my asking?"

"I don't mind at all. My wife and I have the

~ ☾ ~

Generation-2 right now. It's presently nonfunctional."

"We get a lot of customers in here looking to replace the Gen-2. It was a sophisticated model when it came out, but it can't accommodate the new software patches. You need a bigger hard drive. That's reality. It's hard to keep up with technology."

Stanford looked back at the display case to examine the features on the aides. "What about a dust trap?"

"These units have an internal vaporizer for dust and pet dander. Do you have pets?"

"Yes, a border collie."

"All the more reason for the vaporizer," said the android. "Pet dander is a major culprit for hardware malfunctions – that and overheating. The advanced features in the HE models will ensure that you have all your bases covered, and they come with an extended warranty."

"How much do they go for?"

"You're looking into the high nineties."

"What about less pricey versions?"

"Follow me," said the android.

They climbed aboard the cart again and drove further into the bowels of the store. When they reached the escalator the cart stopped, and Stanford followed the android up to the second story on foot, through more aisles displaying various generations of robot aides and accessories. Most of the accessories were completely foreign to him – strange shapes and designs that he had never seen.

It was noticeably dimmer at the far end of the store. Several EM tubes flickered in the ceiling, needing to be swapped out.

"These are the refurbished models. They are still high efficiency with a lot of the same features as the new generation, but with a slightly smaller CPU. It will still do what you want but without all the bells and whistles. This is what I'd recommend if you are on a budget."

~ ☾ ~

The aides in this section were duller and appeared second rate. It was clear they were not given the same care as the more expensive models.

The android salesman seemed to notice that Stanford was less than impressed.

"Alternately," said the android, "you can bring in your existing Gen-2 for a maintenance assessment. We can hook it up to our diagnostic equipment and scan for the fault. But, if you want my honest opinion, you should consider upgrading. Once an aide starts to show signs of age, it's just a matter of time until it ultimately crashes. That's my best advice."

"I don't know."

Stanford glanced at the piles of robot parts in the big mesh bin next to him. There were skulls with blank eyes staring back, appendages reaching out to him, and torsos with circuitry poking out where the legs should be. He felt the urge to leave the store at once.

He turned to the salesman. "Thank you for your time," he said. "You've given me a lot to think about. I'd like to go back to my wife and tell her what I've seen. She'll have a lot of input into the final decision. Ultimately, the aide has to match her needs more than mine."

"That's a smart move, Mr.?"

"Samuels."

The salesman reached into a pouch in his overalls and removed a business card. The card read: *Reece, Synthetic. Sales Executive, RE Corporation.*

Stanford took the card. "You're a synthetic."

"Couldn't you tell?"

"I suspected but—"

"—But it's never obvious, I know what you mean. I can barely tell myself anymore. The truth is that I'm a synthetic with a beautiful woman partner in the northeast quadrant."

"A human?"

~ ☾ ~

"A mutant, yes. We're very happy. Even if my wife were to find a match, we'd stay together. We believe in the Policy, but we are happy as we are."

"Is it common for mutants to couple with androids?"

"It's more common than you know. Mutants are tired of living as solitaries, and it doesn't defy the Policy because androids are not designed to procreate."

"Doesn't your wife fear permanent midnight?"

"Of course she does. But she's been registered for coupling for years and it hasn't happened yet. Let me ask you a question, Mr. Samuels: Would you rather wait all alone for something that may never happen or be together with the woman you love in the dark?"

Stanford could see emotion welling in the android's eyes.

It's remarkable, he thought, *this robot is capable of sharing the human experience. He connects to a human being as if he is one himself.*

"It was good to meet you, Reece," said Stanford. "I'll be in touch."

"Come again, Mr. Samuels. Good luck with your decision."

Stanford looked around at the miles of aisles and then back at the robot.

"How do I get out of here?"

The android laughed. "Follow me."

~ ☾ ~

2.95 (ELECTRIC FERN)

It was only half a block outside the Emporium that Stanford saw the green haze of a photon glare out a storefront window. As he passed through the swath on the sidewalk, he couldn't help but look inside at the beautiful electric fern in the display case. He was trapped.

The fern noticed him immediately, beckoning with its large feathery fronds. It seemed to know how much he desired it; within moments the fern convinced him to place his palms on the pane of glass to make a connection. Stanford felt heat transferring through the window, radiating all the way down his arms and into his chest.

The plant was excited by his presence, moving faster and more seductively in the pot, drawing him further into its influence. The lure of sleep pulled at Stanford's eyelids. Quite suddenly, the sensation of a sharp slap across his face sent a painful shockwave through his jawbone all the way to his temples. Had he been slapped by the frond through the glass?

He recoiled and stumbled backwards. When his eyes refocused, he was no longer on the street. He found himself standing in the center of a massive landscape that stretched as far as he could see.

Where am I? Where have you transported me?

He knew instantly that he was in a dream, as the bizarre images came to him the way they did each time the sleep transmitter was set too high. But the dream was lucid, more so than other dreams. Looking in every direction, there were no buildings, no walls separating

~ ☾ ~

the colonies, no signs of civilization. He was standing in a vast field of aquamarine. Millions upon millions of tangled ferns sprouted through acres of top soil. Everywhere he looked, the ferns were vibrant green, all shapes and sizes, and so numerous they choked out every other form of plant life. It was remarkable to see so much vegetation in one place, thriving in the contaminated soil. He was eager to experience the sensations of organic life.

He knelt down to touch a single feathery leaf. It was soft and fragile. It had no resemblance to the artificial plants he kept at home. His curiosity intensified. He began to dig around the base of the stem to see what fed it, shifting the ashen soil to the side in a pile.

The root system was uncovered before long. He took hold of the stem and pulled it from its resting place. It was more difficult than he imagined; the roots crackled as they were torn from the ground, and screams of agony rose up from the face of Ultim.

With the severed plant in his grasp, a bolt of electricity shot through his arm, and then there was only blackness ...

When he opened his eyes, he was back on the street under the awning, faces belonging to paramedics standing over him.

He tried to lift his head off the sidewalk but there was too much pain.

"Don't move your head," the closest paramedic said. "You could have a neck injury."

"Where are my sunglasses?"

A second medic arrived with a spine board. "Your eyes are on fire."

"Where are my glasses?" Stanford repeated.

"We'll find them. Just don't move. We're going to get you on the spinal board. We need to immobilize your neck."

~ ☾ ~

One of the medics stabilized Stanford's chin while the other rolled his body just enough so the board could be placed beneath his back. As his body was adjusted, Stanford caught a glimpse of the fern in the window. It was dormant now. The leaves appeared droopy and wilted. The once vibrant color had become dull.

The medics strapped his arms, torso, legs, and forehead to the spinal board so he couldn't move any part of his body.

I'm a prisoner, he thought. *Where are you taking me?*

"Where are you taking me?" he said aloud.

"Try not to talk. You might be in shock."

"I need to call my wife."

"It's all taken care of, mister. Just relax. We'll take things from here. You've got nothing to worry about."

"I was devoured by ferns."

The first medic looked at the second. "He's in shock."

"The ferns were everywhere. Some were ten feet tall. They had taken over; they were in charge. There was nothing left."

~ ☾ ~

3.0

The outdoor café in the central sector was bustling with mutant customers. Sarah sat under an umbrella at a small round table, glancing towards the gated entrance expectantly. A family at a nearby table caught her attention. She watched two small children fussing with their food while the parents seemed completely oblivious. The adults smiled and laughed as they conversed, as any parents of two eradicated children would. What wasn't there to be happy about? A table of four had been reserved for their family in Salus; their future was guaranteed.

How would they feel the day their children turned five years old and were dropped off at the donation stations? Would they be devastated about their family being ripped apart or would they be joyous that they had served the Policy? Would they make promises to reunite in the dome after the suns burned out?

Sarah felt a fluttering sensation in her stomach as she watched the children fidget in their seats like little bundles of kinetic energy. The little girl with dark braids and the runt of a boy with feathery brown tufts over his ears would be welcome additions to the Perfect colony. How desperately she longed for a day when she could bring her own child to the café.

Sarah was so lost in thought that she barely noticed her friend sitting down in the chair across the table from her.

"Sarah?" The woman wore a sun hat with a floppy brim that partly obscured her neatly applied eyeliner and radiant purple mascara. "Are you okay?"

~ ☾ ~

Sarah focused her eyes and smiled. "I'm fine, Audrey. I was just daydreaming. You know how it is."

Audrey chuckled as she set her overly inflated purse on the ground next to her chair. "I sure do." The woman was one part excited, the other part scatterbrained. "Have you been waiting long?"

"Not long at all. I just arrived."

"Oh good. The traffic is so heavy it's almost impossible to get anywhere on time. And I found this darling market that I just had to stop at. Look what I got."

Audrey reached into her bag and revealed a package of vibrant orange carrots.

"They're from Salus. Look at how beautiful they are. The vendor said the vegetables from the greenhouses don't come close to the genuine produce being harvested in the environment. He said they literally burst with flavor."

She handed the package across the table.

Sarah sniffed inside, taking in the fresh aroma.

"They will be perfect in stew. Oh, Sarah, let me take you there! I need to show you all the wondrous produce! It's amazing!"

Sarah smiled.

"Oh, darling, I'm sorry." Audrey stuffed the carrots back in her purse. "I'm just so excited. I'm being terribly rude. Have you ordered?"

"Not yet."

Audrey waved the waitress over and each woman ordered a cool cocktail. Sarah felt a sense of relief that her friend was so outgoing. That way she could just relax and sink into the background.

"The suns are so hot," said Audrey with a dramatic flair. "I can barely stand to be outside for more than a few minutes."

"Do you want to move inside?"

"You're so sweet, Sarah, but I'll be fine. Let's just

~ ☾ ~

stick to the indoor malls today, if you don't mind. After
I take you to the market, of course."

"Of course."

The woman suddenly leaned close. Sarah could see
the heavy powder on her cheeks.

"It seems like forever since I saw you, dear. What
have you been up to? How are you and Stanford?"

"Everything is fine, Audrey. Nothing much changes."

Audrey leaned back and thinned her eyes to
emphasize her dubious expression. "Are you sure
everything is okay?"

"I'm fine, really." Sarah shifted in her seat,
uncomfortable with the scrutiny.

"I know you, Sarah. It takes an Eradicator to know an
Eradicator." She jutted in close again and snatched up
Sarah's hand. "Your time will come, my dear. It
happened for me and it will happen to you. Don't be
hard on yourself. Worrying won't make it come any
faster."

"I don't know what you mean."

"Oh, come now. I can read you like a book, friend."

Sarah smiled sheepishly and glanced at the children
at the nearby table again. When she turned back to her
friend she said, "Let's have a nice day, okay?"

Audrey pumped her fists in the air. "I'm ready to
paint this town red if you are!"

Sarah laughed. Audrey's exuberance always had a
way of lifting her spirits. She needed this time to
escape more than anything. It would do her a world of
good.

"Can I ask you something? Then I won't talk about it
anymore for the rest of the day. I promise."

"Of course, darling." Audrey tilted her head again so
the brim of her hat hid her brightly-colored eye
makeup. "You can ask me anything."

Sarah hesitated a moment. "How did it feel to give up
Michael for adoption?"

~ ☾ ~

The woman was silent for a time before a wide smile etched across her face.

"It was wonderful, Sarah. Giving up Michael was an honor for William and me. What more can a mother ask for than to have the opportunity to serve the Policy? You will get your turn soon, I know it."

At that moment the waitress arrived with the cold drinks. Sarah took a sip from her straw and immediately wished she hadn't asked the question.

"Why did you ask me that, Sarah?"

"Oh ... I was just wondering if it was hard. It seems like it might be very hard to part with your child. Who knows when you'll see him again?"

Audrey's smile never wavered. "It's not a hard thing to do when you are an Eradicator serving the Patron. It's easy because it's the right thing to do. It's for the good of our race. It's good for William and me. I know my family will be reunited in Salus when the time comes. You know that as well as I, Sarah."

"I know. But don't you wish you could be together now?"

Audrey scrunched her nose. "I knew the moment I was chosen as an Eradicator that my duty was to be here and have as many children with my couplet as I could. Michael is in their care now, Sarah. Why are you doubting the Policy?"

Sarah shrugged. "I'm not doubting, Audrey. I'm just thinking out loud."

"You're thinking too much. Your mind is clouded. Things will become clear for you in time."

"I guess only a mother would know."

"Oh, Sarah, please! You'll be a mother before you know it. Don't worry. Maybe you should just focus on your love for Stanford right now and things will fall into place."

Sarah managed a smile.

"Now let's talk about that darling market with all the

~ ☾ ~

fresh produce. Turn that frown upside down!"

Sarah glanced back at the children. The parents continued to chatter and laugh, totally oblivious of the two small miracles who sat at their table. She wondered why the couplet didn't pay more attention to the children, knowing their time together was finite. They seemed so happy with the arrangement.

She glanced back at Audrey's smiling face. It seemed everybody around her was quite happy indeed.

~ ☾ ~

3.2

Stanford was strapped firmly to the examination table with a medical imaging machine positioned above him. The machine roved over his entire length, photographing the interior of his body, before retracting on a robotic arm and disappearing into the ceiling.

Stanford tried to turn his neck but he was immobile; he felt groggy and disoriented. Out the corner of his eye he saw the doctor wander in and sit in front of a large computer monitor.

"Where am I?" His voice was weak and barely audible.

The doctor looked over. "You're awake. Try to remain still. You bumped your head when you hit the sidewalk."

"How did I fall?"

The doctor was focused on the monitor. "Liver function has diminished since last time we checked. There's evidence of new scar tissue."

Cross examining new photos with images from previous exams, he continued, "How many times have you fainted before today?"

"I don't remember fainting today."

"Do you remember fainting prior to today?"

"No."

"So today was the first?"

"Like I said, I don't remember."

The doctor inputted the information into a database.

"What are you typing? Why won't you tell me what happened?"

The doctor turned to face him. "Cirrhosis is not the culprit. I mean, your liver didn't cause you to faint. I'm

~ ☾ ~

going to increase your dose of copper-binders to see if we can get more of it out of your urine. I don't like the rate of fibrosis. There could be complications."

"What kind of complications?"

"How's your diet, Stanford? Did you eat anything unusual today?"

"What kind of complications?"

The doctor made a dismissive gesture. "It's remote," he said. "Let's focus on what we know for sure. What did you eat today?"

"I had eggs."

"Genuine or artificial?"

"Does it matter?"

"It could."

"They came from the environment," he said. He suddenly remembered his wife preparing breakfast. "I need to call Sarah."

The doctor swiveled back to his computer and made a note on the touch screen. "Your wife has been notified, Stanford. She's been debriefed, and she expects you home very soon."

"How soon?"

"We're not going to keep you overnight. We've got what we need. Now, I want you to avoid eggs in general. I also recommend that you stay away from nuts, shellfish, mushrooms, anything containing high doses of copper. We want to flush as much as we can from your system to slow the degeneration. I can get the office to make you a food list."

"Why did I faint?"

"I'll need to analyze the data before I can give you a definitive diagnosis. It will take time. How are you feeling otherwise? How's your energy?"

Stanford flinched from a shooting pain in his neck. "I'm tired. But what does that prove other than I'm getting older?"

The doctor grinned. "I'll give you something for your

~ ☾ ~

neck. It's a mild muscle relaxant. You passed the concussion protocol, so there's nothing to worry about there. You'll have a bit of a headache for a couple of days, but it will pass."

The doctor entered a prescription on the touch screen and within moments an injector pen descended from the ceiling on the robotic arm.

"We'll get you started with an intravenous shot to make sure it gets to the bloodstream. You'll feel a little poke."

Stanford tensed as the plunger depressed into his vein and watched the robotic arm return to the ceiling.

"I know this may sound unorthodox, Mr. Samuels, but in addition to increasing your medication, I recommend you seek out an electric fern as a therapeutic option. Now, I'm not a botanist so I can't tell you exactly how these plants do what they do or why they appeared on this planet after the war, but there's proof that spending time with a fern can be beneficial. Domesticated plants are expensive, so I'm not suggesting you go out and purchase one, but there are places that offer affordable 'face time.' You don't need much; just a few minutes a day. Sit next to it, talk to it like it's a person. They are so responsive to human contact, even mimicking human mannerisms, that it won't be a stretch. Let's try getting you back on track. You can get dressed now."

The binding straps retracted, releasing Stanford from the table. Feeling his freedom, he sat up and waited for the dizziness to pass before reaching for his clothes. His sunglasses sat atop the neatly folded pile of laundry.

"Why do I need therapy, Doctor?"

"You're under a lot of stress, Stanford, and therapy is something that can help all of us. It guides us to our center, and it helps calm our mind so our physical body can get right. If the mental is out of line, the physical won't have a chance. Just try it and see how it goes. You

~ ☾ ~

don't have to make a long-term commitment. I mention it only as a suggestion."

Stanford felt a surge of pain in his temple as he recalled the fern in the store window. "I was with a fern right before I fainted."

The doctor took a moment to digest the new information.

"Depending on the size of the plant, you may need to give it some distance. Allow your body to become acquainted with it, and vice versa. This isn't a natural relationship, Stanford – this is man and plant. It's a complex interaction. There are people at the clinics who will counsel you. I'll get a referral and have my office call you at home."

"Can the fern help us get pregnant?"

The doctor looked at him seriously. "You have Wilson's disease, Mr. Samuels. Your liver has nothing to do with reproduction. If you want, I can schedule you another appointment with the fertility clinic, but the previous test results show nothing abnormal with your reproductive capability or with those of your wife. My recommendation is that you continue to refer to the ovulation chart and get yourself in the best shape possible so when conditions are ideal, you are set to produce an offspring with a perfect set of chromosomes. Try to remember that the birth process is still a natural phenomenon, and the Policy is based on probability, not certainty. It can be frustrating, but let's always keep the Policy in mind."

"Of course," said Stanford.

Two bottles of medication shot down the chute and landed at the base of the dispensing machine. The doctor handed them over one at a time.

"This is for your neck, and this is for your liver. We'll see you back here for your next scheduled checkup, Mr. Samuels. I'll get that referral. Try to stay positive. You'd be amazed how negativity can affect the physical body.

~ ☾ ~

And don't worry about today. Things just happen sometimes."

"They just happen? Is that your medical opinion?"

"The human body is a complex organism, Stanford. Even the geneticists have yet to pin it down. You are a wonder of evolution. Have you ever considered how special you are? How many people can claim to have Wilson's disease?"

"I don't know."

"You're the only one in the colony, Stanford. Think about that. It's pretty amazing how unique you are. Of all the mutants with all the thousands of genetic imperfections, you're the only one of your kind."

Stanford finished getting dressed and put on his sunglasses. "It doesn't feel amazing."

The doctor chuckled. "I don't imagine it does at this very moment. You'll feel better soon, Stanford. Go home and get some rest."

~ ☾ ~

3.5 (FERTILITY)

When he returned home Stanford saw a strange man in a white technician's jacket on the walkway in front of his house. He watched the stranger make his way down to a white hover van parked out front. The man looked back at him but said nothing before getting into the vehicle and flying away, as if he were a mirage that had never been there.

"Honey, I was so worried."

The voice belonged to his wife.

"Your work said you didn't show up."

He turned to see her on the stoop. "I was at the hospital," he said.

"I know. A nurse called on the videophone and told me what happened. I wanted to come but they said you were about to be discharged. They said you have a mild concussion and it's nothing much to worry about. I don't know why they didn't call sooner. I was worried sick. How did you fall?"

"I don't remember. I think I was attacked by a plant."

"What?"

Stanford walked up the steps and slipped past her into the foyer. "Who was that man?"

"Stanford, you were attacked by what?"

"I tripped, Sarah." His voice was firm now. "Who was that man?"

She looked frazzled. "He was here for the sleep arc, don't you remember?"

"How did you get an appointment so fast?"

"I called as soon as I got home from shopping with Audrey. They had a cancellation."

~ ☾ ~

Sarah helped him out of his jacket.

"I'm so sorry I wasn't there for you. The nurse on the videophone downplayed it, but I don't know what to think. She said you just need rest. Tell me the truth, are you really okay?"

"What did he say?"

She looked at him curiously. "What did *who* say?"

"The sleep technician."

Sarah shut the front door. "He did a scan of the transmitter but found nothing unusual. He said we should watch the levels and report back if it happens again. He said it just happens sometimes. A current can jump a line and then fix itself within a few moments, but it affects the entire night's transmission. That's probably what happened in this case. But why are you so worried about that right now? You just need to focus on getting better."

"Maybe the faulty transmission is why this all happened in the first place," he said.

"Oh, honey."

She tried to hug him but he recoiled.

"Your neck," she said. "I'm sorry." Tears welled in her perfect brown chestnuts. "Oh, Stanford, I think I may have bumped your setting last night. I wanted to turn it down to see if I could wean you off it, but I must have turned it the wrong way. I'm so sorry. I shouldn't have done that."

Stanford felt a sharp pain blast his temples as he went to retrieve the medication from his jacket. He clenched the bottles tightly in his fists while staring into the closet, not wanting to face her.

"I'm sorry," she said from behind. "I had no right to fiddle with your setting. But please understand, honey, I was trying to help."

She moved in close, placing her trembling hand on his shoulder.

He turned slowly towards her and watched a tear streak down her face.

~ ☽ ~

She struggled to speak. "We're a right mess, aren't we, Stanford?"

He could see by her quivering chin how sorry she was. He felt his anger melting away.

"How's the old boy?" he asked.

"He didn't pee on the floor while you were gone – at least not that I noticed."

"See, things are looking up." He managed a little smile.

"Oh, baby, I'm so sorry. I feel awful for how things turned out. I love you so much."

He embraced her now, smelling a familiar scent.

"You're wearing the perfume I got for your birthday," he said.

She smiled. "Yes. I know you like it."

"I do."

She kissed him on the cheek. "Come," she said, taking the medicine from his hands. "I have something to show you."

When they entered the kitchen he noticed the EM tubes had been dimmed to create a pleasant twilight. He saw a bowl of steaming beef stew on the centerpiece.

"What do you think?" she asked.

"I think I love you."

She laughed. "You must have taken an awful bump. What about the beef?"

"I love that, too."

"So you forgive me?"

"Of course I forgive you, Sarah."

He kissed her and approached the table. There were carrots mixed with the cubes of beef and gravy and other pieces of vegetable that he longed to get in his mouth. He hadn't tasted a genuine vegetable since the farmland had been contaminated.

"Are they imported from the artificial environment?"

"Just the vegetables," she said. "All the vendors are selling them now."

~ ☾ ~

They sat down, and she served the stew.

"This is delicious," he said. "I almost forgot what real meat tastes like."

"The beef isn't genuine, darling."

"The eggs are genuine but not the cattle?"

"It will come," she said. "Be patient."

He smiled across the table, but couldn't hide his fatigue any longer. As much as he wanted to enjoy the meal, he was losing the battle with exhaustion. He felt his body go limp. The medication made him nauseous.

"Let's go, Stanford," she said. "You need to rest. We can have this tomorrow."

He was only semi-conscious as his wife led him down the dark corridor towards the bedroom. She sat him on the edge of the bed and ran her hand soothingly through his hair.

"You've had such a day," she said. "I'll set the transmitter."

He watched her approach the black box on the bedside table and set the dial. An arc of white light immediately beamed from the box, arching over the bed and creating a low hum that pacified his mind.

She turned to face him. "Do you need my help getting undressed?"

He stared into her chestnut eyes. She did so much to please him.

"No, I'm okay."

"Okay, honey. I'm going to take a quick shower in the condensation booth. I'll tuck you in when I get back, okay?"

"Okay," he said.

He watched her disappear into the en suite and just as he was about to lie back on the bed he felt the old collie rubbing affectionately against his ankles. He leaned forward to see the black and white blob nestling between his feet on the floor.

"Remember the collie farm," he said. "You owe me a

~ ☾ ~

lifetime of service, old boy. You just have a bit of incontinence, is all; no more than that. You'll be just fine."

He tried to remove his pants, but the effort was too great. Every muscle in his body seemed to have lost power. Giving up, he rested his head on the pillow and pulled the sheets over his clothed body. He watched the stream of light beam intensely overhead. The continuous hum from the transmitter lulled him to the edge of consciousness, but he was pulled back by the sound of his wife weeping from the en suite.

It took all he had to get out of bed and approach the closed door. He leaned close to listen. "Can I come in?"

Receiving no answer he made the decision to enter.

There she was, head down, slumped on the toilet seat with the pregnancy monitor dangling between her fingers.

She focused her weepy eyes on him. "What's wrong with us?" she said.

Stanford watched her silently from the doorway. He had no words.

She spoke again. "We were coupled for a reason, Stanford. We need to eradicate your eyes and produce a normal child. We have no other purpose. If we don't, we'll die here."

"We have each other, Sarah."

She began to cry. "Oh ... God help us."

He stepped forward but she raised her hand. "I need a moment alone," she said.

"Do you want me to close the door?"

"Yes."

Back in the bedroom he knelt next to the sleeping collie and ran his hand along the length of the old boy's back, following the nodules of the spine down to the tip of the tail.

Of every relationship I've ever had, you are the longest lasting and most stable, old boy. Do you

~ ☾ ~

remember when I picked you off the farm? My mom brought me there on my fifth birthday. I picked you out of hundreds. We were destined to be together from that moment, you and I. My mother wanted me to give you a name, but I wanted to call you 'old boy.' I don't know why. I just liked the sound of it. And you know what? I don't regret it, old boy. There is no name that is good enough for you. Sweet dreams, old boy.

Stanford crawled into bed and pulled up the sheets. He didn't bother to get undressed.

~ ☾ ~

4.0

A few minutes in the condensation booth was enough to remove any lingering residue from the day before. After dressing in his overalls, Stanford went to the kitchen where his wife had set the table with a simple breakfast of cold cereal and powdered milk.

"You look energized, Stanford."

"Thank you. You look lovely."

She kissed his cheek and went to fetch the thermos from the brewer.

"Did you dream?"

Stanford looked at her and smiled. "Yes, but nothing linear."

"That's good. It means your hormones are back in balance."

"Yes."

"I'm so glad the transmission is back to normal."

"I am too."

He could tell she was in better spirits today. Her movements were dainty again; her skin had a healthy sheen. There was no evidence of the broken woman from the night before.

"Did you sleep well?" he asked.

"Like a log. I even remember my dream."

He watched her for a moment. "Do you want to tell me about it?"

"Do you really want to hear it?"

"If you want to tell me, then yes, I'd like to hear it."

"But my dream is my own, Stanford."

"You're right, I'm sorry."

He watched her face soften and produce a cheeky

~ ☾ ~

grin. "I'm kidding. I want to share it with you. I don't mind."

"If you feel comfortable, I would love to hear it."

She brought the thermos to the table and filled both their mugs before taking her place. He could tell there was a sense of excitement that jumped around inside her.

"There was a nature reserve in the northern quadrant of the Perfect colony," she said, "surrounded by massive trees before the war."

"You remember back that far?"

"I remember some things; little snippets of memories. My imagination fills in the blanks."

Stanford smiled. "Go on."

"My mother used to take me there when I was a little girl. I remember how I would hold her hand when we walked along the path through the forest towards the picnic tables. There was a smell – some weird organic mixture like tree bark and rotting leaves that rose up from the ground. If you knelt down to touch the soil you could feel heat emanating from underground. Most people said it stank of decay – said they wished it would be restaged like the other artificial parks, but I loved it because it was unique to that place. It seemed so magical, like a fairy tale. That smell was all a part of the charm. I remember it vividly. But it wasn't just the smell. It was everything; the trees were so majestic, like giants from another time. It's the only place I had ever seen such tall trees and never again since." She paused in thought. "I can even hear the sound of my mother's laughter when I asked her if the trees held up the sky."

Stanford watched a smile etch across her face as the memory crystallized.

"Did you see any wildlife?" he asked after a moment.

She was deep in thought now.

"There were lots of creatures up there at that time. They mostly hid during the daylight hours, sleeping in

~ ☾ ~

their burrows and waiting for nightfall, but I saw deer a few times, and many different species of birds. I remember my mother bought me a bird book for my birthday so I could identify the different types each time we went up. It was something we did together." She paused. "I don't know where that book went. It probably burned with everything else."

She was silent as the images fluttered in her consciousness.

"Anyway, that was my dream. Nothing spectacular happened. I just wandered through the pathway with my mother, smelling those scents, seeing those trees, hearing the sounds of branches crackling beneath my feet, feeling her hand in mine, and then I woke up and I felt so happy. It was like I was there again. Like really there."

"That sounds pretty spectacular to me."

She smiled. "It is, isn't it? It was wonderful. It makes me feel so good. I wish every dream could be like that."

"Thank you for sharing it with me."

"I'm glad I did," she said. "If I'm going to share my dreams, I want it to be with you."

He watched the emotion well up in her eyes as she took a sip of coffee. Then she looked at him like her mood had been reset. "I've been thinking about that food list," she said. "I'm going to call the clinic this morning before I head into town to pick up some groceries that are safe for you to eat."

He was taken aback by the sudden change of direction. "The list might not be ready yet, Sarah."

"How long can it take, Stanford? We need to start on a new regimen immediately."

"I'm just saying they may not have had time to fill it out. It hasn't even been twenty-four hours. I'm not the only patient at the clinic."

She looked at him silently for a moment and stood up and walked across the kitchen towards the cupboard.

~ ☾ ~

He knew he had upset her. He watched her hand shake as she retrieved a water glass from the cupboard and held it under the spout of the desalinization cooler.

He stood from the table and went to help.

"I'm sorry. Let me hold your hand steady."

When the glass was full she looked at him. "I'm going to call the clinic about the food list," she said, determined.

"I appreciate that," he said.

"You need to take your pills."

"Thanks for reminding me. I'll take them now."

He accepted the glass of purified water and walked back down the hall to the en suite. When he arrived he set the glass on the counter and looked at his reflection in the mirror. The copper was moving around his pupils like the beginning of a storm.

Is this what she sees, he thought, *an ugly man with mutant eyes? How can she accept a man like me? Is that what I am, a man? I look more like a beast. She has no hope for salvation.*

He swallowed the capsules one at a time.

I don't deserve her.

He turned away from his reflection and walked back down the hall. When he reached the foyer he saw the old collie yawn and slump lazily by the front door.

His wife helped him into his jacket and straightened the collar.

"Can I call you at work?" she asked.

"Of course you can."

For a brief moment he considered telling her about his trip to the Robot Emporium, but decided it would be better to surprise her.

"What will you do until the clinic opens?" he asked.

"The condensation booth could use a scrub."

"Good idea," he said. He gave her a kiss on the forehead.

"Don't forget to take your pills again at lunch."

~ ☾ ~

He patted the bottles in his breast pocket.

"What about your glasses?"

He patted the other pocket.

She waited while he put them on. She wouldn't let him get away with anything.

The foyer went instantly dark behind the double-tinted lenses.

"Where did you go?" he joked. Then he turned around and opened the front door. "It's a beautiful day," he said, stepping onto the porch under the dawning light of the twin suns. He felt the heat on his cheeks.

Before he was down the walkway he heard his wife call from the front door.

"Stanford?"

He turned. She looked so hopeful on the porch, putting on her best smile.

"I'm happy for our coupling," she said.

He gave her a little wave. "I am too," he said.

When he reached the sidewalk he paused briefly to glance back, but the front door was closed; the porch was bare.

He felt a pang of sadness. He wished she was still there so he could tell her he loved her.

~ ☾ ~

4.1

As Stanford crossed the platform near the donation station he saw a boy standing in line with his parents on either side. The boy had all the markings of a perfect set of chromosomes: brown eyes, brown hair; clear complexion.

His mother had brown hair, his father blond. Stanford couldn't be sure at this distance what color their eyes were. Other than recessive genes, it was not obvious what mutation the father carried, but whatever it was had surely been eradicated in the offspring.

He watched the child embrace both of his parents before bravely placing his hand into the hand of the Militia man. As the boy reached the gate, two geneticists rushed out to meet him. After a brief examination in which the boy's mouth was swabbed and the saliva tested in a portable thermal cylinder, the men in white coats sent the boy back into the waiting arms of his parents. The mother broke into uncontrolled sobs.

The loud speaker above the gate crackled: *"Not eradicated. Not eradicated ..."*

The father placed his arms around his wife and son and led them back towards the gate of the fusion train. His shoulders were slumped like a man defeated.

The commuters on the platform ignored the message as if it were none of their business.

When the train arrived, Stanford's curiosity got the better of him and he followed the boy and his parents into the rear compartment. The seats filled quickly so he was unable to sit as close to the family as he wanted. He had no desire to speak to them, only to get a sense of

~ ☾ ~

what it was like to fail the Policy. What was the next course of action? Would they try again immediately or would they update their coupling profile and apply for a new match? Would the couplet love their child or would they treat him differently now that they knew he would not lead them to Salus?

Stanford's seat was too far away. He would have to live with his own speculation.

As the train lifted off the tracks he got comfortable in the clamshell. The ride was smooth, and it didn't take long before he felt his eyelids getting heavy. He allowed himself to drift off, picturing his beautiful wife in his mind's eye. She was draped in a white cotton nightgown that clung to every splendid curve. It was the nightgown she wore to bed on special occasions; the one he loved because it was cinched in all the right places. The material was snug against her waist, tightly pressing the mounds of her breasts. He reached out to embrace her but she moved away, backing into darkness until she was swallowed by the recesses of his mind.

Stirring in sleep, Stanford was invaded by a new image. Now he saw a wide open field, gently rolling in all directions as far as the eye could see. There was no sign of civilization in any direction. The only thing existing here were ferns that grew in such abundance they covered the landscape in a brilliant sea of green.

Stanford watched himself from above. He saw his physical body standing in the midst of the ocean of ferns. He was concerned for a moment that the plants might swallow him up. With the suns at their peak, it was strange that he wasn't wearing sunglasses.

In a moment Stanford felt his body drifting upwards like a helium balloon. Farther and farther away he floated into the atmosphere, until his ethereal self tugged with such force that he jolted into the darkness of another unknown place ...

~ ☾ ~

His eyes snapped open, and he saw the passengers retrieving their luggage from overhead compartments. A wave of disorientation washed over him as he came back from sleep. He reached up to feel his glasses. He was in real time now, back in the clamshell seat on the commuter train. The last remnants of the dream petered out like a moth fluttering through his subconscious.

Out the side window of the fusion train he saw mutants exiting onto the platform. Only when the train was completely evacuated did Stanford feel he could make his way down the aisle towards the exit.

~ ☾ ~

4.2 (THE FACTORY)

The industrial sector had been beaten by insurgent bombs during the nuclear war to stem the flow of goods to the Perfect colony. The factories were tired but reliable, continuously pumping out plumes of unfiltered emissions in the process of manufacturing the planet's ores. The sky over the sector was locked under a perpetual state of haze that screened out the twin suns. Centralizing industry to this sector assured pristine air quality beyond the walls in the Perfect colony. Lessons from the devastation of previous planets were not a concern here – not with the construction of Salus nearly complete. The desire for fuel and for material things remained as strong as it always had been for the human race. The planet was a resource that could be exploited from now until the suns burned out, without fear of consequence. The dome was salvation.

Stanford entered the fortified gates, erected during wartime to maintain the security of the factory's operations, and strode up the walkway to the front doors of the battered warehouse. The structure was one of the oldest and most important in the colony, home to hundreds of mutant laborers. The majority of goods manufactured in the mutant colony were shipped here and distributed to the other side of the walls, which had made it a key target for the terrorist attacks.

He strode through the front passageway towards the picking stations and over to the wide-open cement floor of the central loading bay, which was stacked to the ceiling with old wooden storage shelves. A giant bay door was kept closed except for when the pallets were

~ ☾ ~

offloaded into heavily armed delivery trucks.

From the shipping bay he took the service elevator to the second floor and crossed through the receiving dock, just as large as the bay on the first floor, with a similar hanging door that remained closed except for early morning arrivals. Both floors were identical in layout with the exception of the bank of cubicles in the northeast corner of the upper floor. The shipping and receiving bays were busy with mutants and machinery around the clock, creating a thick and muggy atmosphere inside the warehouse.

When Stanford arrived at his processing cubicle, he found a stack of purchase orders on his desk. The pile was double the size of normal due to his absence the previous day. He moved half the stack to the floor to give himself space to work, and activated the SAD light on the corner of his desk. The prism-shaped diode compensated for the diminishing capabilities of the twin suns to provide essential spectral light. The twins had grown hotter over the years as they neared their end, but were less beneficial to the planet's life forms. Stanford stared into the light, allowing the diode to send a vitamin-enriched beam to the back of his eyes, instantly improving his mood.

No longer overwhelmed by his workload, he glanced at the first purchase order. The order sheet was for six handcrafted aluminum pendants. Aluminum was a rare commodity on Ultim, and he wished he could physically touch the items, to feel them in his hands, but the boxes were sealed with hermetic postal straps that could only be released by a sample of the intended recipient's DNA. All genetic samples were registered in the central computer.

Stanford opened the depository drawer where the day's packages awaited shipping labels. The parcel of pendants was destined for a place called: "Idyllic Avenue."

~ ☾ ~

It made him feel happy to think of living on a street with such a name. He wondered what it would be like to be a resident of Idyllic Avenue – to receive a package of luxury aluminum pendants. He thought about living in a house on Idyllic Avenue with Sarah.

He affixed the shipping label and took it to the delivery chute on the opposing wall. Once the chute was opened, a vacuum snatched the box from his hand and sent it on its way to Idyllic Avenue.

Just like that, the first purchase order was processed. He stamped the order paper with company ink and placed the sheet in the out box. Having completed the transaction, he returned to his desk and removed a business card from the pocket of his overalls. He played with the card in his fingers for a moment, thinking about how desperately he wanted to make her happy, before picking up the videophone and dialing ...

A representative of the Robot Emporium came on the screen. "How can I help you?"

"Hello, I'd like to speak to a customer service representative called Reece."

"One moment, please."

The face disappeared from the videophone. Stanford felt an anxious sensation inside that made him shift in his seat. The decision had been made. He could picture his wife's excitement as the aide walked through the door. The steel plating would be freshly polished and glisten under the EM tubes in the foyer. Her brown chestnut eyes would swell with tears of joy as he explained all the high tech features that the new generation model had to offer. He hadn't done nearly enough for her. She deserved this.

The face of Reece appeared on the screen. "Hello, Mr. Samuels. It's nice to see you again."

"Likewise."

"I'm eager to hear what you've decided."

"I want to go with the Gen-3."

~ ☾ ~

"The refurbished unit?"

"No, the new model."

"That's an excellent choice, Mr. Samuels, but I assumed you were on a budget."

"I am. I can put in extra hours at the factory. I have been thinking about what you said about your wife and how much you would do for her. I want to do something for Sarah."

"Mr. Samuels, it would be my honor to assist you. You are doing a wonderful thing."

"Thank you, Reece."

"If you are going with the Gen-3, may I suggest you upgrade to the unit with the *broca* chip? It's the most advanced unit on the market."

"What's a broca chip?"

"It's a chip installed in the CPU that gives the aide superior aural and verbal skills. The advanced linguistic capabilities significantly reduce the potential for misinterpretation of commands. A common complaint with the former models was that they had to be told several times to carry out a duty. That's not the case with models that have been installed with the broca. Their ability to understand language and react to commands is as good as yours or mine."

"Give me the broca chip, Reece."

The android smiled. "Excellent. I'll put a unit on order and it will be shipped out on a priority pod in seven to ten business days. And how will you be paying, Mr. Samuels?"

Stanford flashed his titanium transaction card in front of the screen and inserted it into a slot in the videophone.

"Payment received, Mr. Samuels. It has been my pleasure. I know your wife will be thrilled with the Gen-3."

"Thank you, Reece. It's been a pleasure to meet you."

"Have a wonderful day, Mr. Samuels."

~ ☾ ~

"Goodbye."

Stanford hung up the receiver and took a deep breath. He looked at the wall clock. It was nowhere near break time. The stack of orders on his desk was only smaller by one.

He thought more about what it must be like on Idyllic Avenue.

~ ☾ ~

4.3

When break time finally arrived, mutants flooded into the cafeteria and claimed their seats.

Stanford located the old man with haemochromatosis and sat down across the table. Stanford and the old man shared a disease of mineral overload – Stanford's from copper, the old man's from iron.

The old man smiled. "Hello, Saturn."

"Hi, Iron Man."

The old man laughed like he always did when they referred to one another by their nicknames. "I ate alone yesterday."

"I had a dentist appointment," returned Stanford.

"Got any cavities?"

"Not one."

"Show me your pearly whites."

Stanford bared his teeth and chuckled.

"How's Sarah?"

"She's good. I ordered her a new robot aide. I'm going to have it delivered."

"Is it her birthday?"

"No, it's just a surprise."

"What are you making up for?"

Stanford smiled. "I just want to give her something – to repay her for her sacrifice as my Eradicator."

The old man sat in ponderous silence. "She's lucky to have you, Saturn." He took a sip of his coffee. "You should go away with her. Take her someplace nice."

"Some place like Idyllic Avenue?"

"Where is that?"

~ ☾ ~

"I have no idea," said Stanford.

The old man shrugged. "I envy you, Stanford. She's a lovely woman."

He could see the man's eyes well up with tears.

They sat in silence now, sipping coffee and glancing around at the different factions of mutants who filled the tables. The albinos sat together, as did the Downs, the manic depressives, the web-toes, and so on, all keeping with their kind. There was no rule requiring like mutants to sit together in the mess hall, but that's how it always went. Mutants felt most comfortable consorting with those who shared their disease. Those who shared their disease also shared their pain.

Stanford's mutation was such a rarity that he shared his disease with no one; the old man was as close to a genetic connection as it got. As for the old man, he preferred to stay away from the others with haemochromatosis. He said it was because they were moody when they were low on iron. He had worked in the factory longer than anyone, and over the years he had gained the reputation as a loner. That was until Stanford arrived. Now the two men had grown close and always made sure the other didn't eat alone. Each man made work a little more tolerable for the other.

The old man settled his eyes back on Stanford. "You got something on your mind, Saturn?"

Stanford looked back. "Not really."

"You seem like you're daydreaming."

"Maybe I am a little." Stanford smiled.

"You have it okay, Saturn. Your time will come. You're a good man."

"The good men are on the other side of the walls. Good men are the ones who serve the Policy."

The old man slammed his fist on the table. "Don't insult me, Stanford. I've been living as a solitary my whole life. I'm a good man. And I know a good one

~ ☾ ~

when I see one. Being good has nothing to do with delivering babies!"

The old man ruminated in silence for a moment. He had a faraway look in his tired old eyes. When he focused on Stanford again he said, "You hear about Ian from the picking department?" His voice was considerably calmer now.

"I don't know him."

"Sure you do. He's the one with Klinefelter's syndrome. His nickname is XXY. He sits over at that table with those others."

Stanford looked over at the table with the other Klinefelters and nodded in vague recollection. "What about him?"

"Got picked up yesterday, copulating with another mutant. Now there's a man who has problems."

"I didn't hear that. Surely he knows it's against the Policy."

"Of course he does. Everybody knows it, Saturn. But it's a load of hogwash in this case, you know."

"How's that?"

"Klinefelter's can't procreate. They're infertile."

"How do you know?"

The old man gave Stanford a look and glanced at the clock above the buffet tables that were being prepared for lunch.

"It's time for my bloodletting," said the old man. "See you at lunch, Stanford."

The entire mess hall began filing out at the same time to return to work. When Stanford arrived back at his cubicle he saw the amber light flashing above the depository tray to indicate that a package had arrived. He opened the tray and removed a note from inside.

"Stanford Samuels. The hospital called. Your wife has been in an accident."

Stanford rushed from the cubicle, shooting down the service elevator and crossing the shipping bay towards

~ ☾ ~

the front doors. As he ran blindly across the street towards the terminal, luckily avoiding the steady traffic of hover cars, one word continued to echo through his mind over and over.

Sarah ... Sarah ... Sarah ...

~ ☾ ~

4.5

He sat completely still in the rear compartment of the fusion train, oblivious of the mutants who gawked at his emotional collapse. Perhaps it was a coping mechanism that caused his brain to suddenly recall meeting his wife for the first time. The location had been Hotel Grand in the western quadrant. Every so often when the genetics division discovered a windfall of Eradicators, they would hold a coupling ball to celebrate their hard work in style. Perfects, selected for their corrective genes, would be trotted out before the men and women whose mutations were the most perplexing in the colony.

The balls were always a formal affair, so Stanford sat uncomfortably in a rented tuxedo with the rest of the mutant bachelors on one side of the ballroom, while the bachelorettes were ushered out through a curtain on the opposite end. The Perfects walked with an air of confidence that came from knowing the geneticists would take care of them tonight; the pressure that came from being selected an Eradicator would be alleviated the moment they were matched with their couplet. From then on, the anxiety they felt would melt away in an instant, and they could concentrate solely on the single goal of serving the Policy.

Stanford was immediately drawn to a brown-haired woman who walked gracefully along the stage in a red fitted dress. She was a beautiful creature unlike any other he had encountered, and he desperately hoped she was the one. Her long hair dropped down across her shoulders like woven silk. He couldn't take his eyes off her as she made her way across the floor towards his

~ ☾ ~

table, her shapely sleek legs seeming to cut the distance
of the floor in half with each stride.

All of the mutants jumped from their seats when she
arrived. She glanced at each of them with indifference
and then looked at her ticket.

"My ticket says 'Stanford Samuels,'" she said. Her
voice was like the powdery wings of a moth. "Is one of
you him?"

Stanford felt a wave of adrenaline rush through his
entire body.

"Yes," he said. "I'm him."

"His nickname is Saturn," said the mutant with the
widow's peak standing next to Stanford.

The beautiful woman smiled and looked directly at
the man called "Saturn."

"I'm Sarah," she said. "This is the part where you ask
me to dance."

"Of course," he said, and he gave her his hand. He
was embarrassed by how sticky his palm had become.

Sarah led him to the dance floor. She placed one of
his unsteady hands on her hip, the other around her
neck, and instructed him how to move. He was glad for
the instruction, as the way he danced felt like his
mutation was a club foot. He tried his best not to step
on her toes. His heart was nearly beating out of his
chest and his breathing was rapid.

"I like your tuxedo," she said.

Stanford was so focused on his footwork that he
barely heard her voice.

"Is it grizzly hair?" she asked.

"What?"

"Is your jacket made of grizzly hair?"

"Oh ... yes."

"It's very becoming, Stanford."

"You look nice too."

Even at close range, she had an immaculate
complexion.

~ ☾ ~

"There's nothing to worry about," she said. "I don't bite."

"That's a relief." He feigned a chuckle and glanced quickly back at his feet.

She smiled. "My dress is made of pelican feathers."

"My jacket is rented."

She laughed and led him in an awkward twirl. "You're a good dancer," she said. "You could use some fine tuning, but you have potential. Most men end up tossing me around like a rag doll, but you're gentle and sweet. Do you take after your mother or your father?"

Stanford thought about it. "My mother, I think. What about you?"

"My father died in the war when I was five, so I guess my mother."

"I'm sorry."

"It's okay. I try not to think about it anymore. Are your folks still alive?"

Stanford shook his head.

"Let's not talk about it. This is a wonderful night, Stanford Samuels."

She picked up the pace, twirling around on the tips of her toes and then coming in close again. "We have the same initials now that we're coupled." She laughed, caught up in the blissful moment.

She looked so beautiful and he suddenly felt happier than he had ever been. But there was still something that made him apprehensive, something he needed to ask.

"Do my eyes make you nervous?"

She paused for a moment to stare into his mutation and said, "Dip me."

Stanford was reluctant, fearful that he might drop her on her head, but she insisted and so he dipped her and when she came back up she wrapped both arms around his neck, graceful as a swan.

"You have beautiful eyes, Stanford, beautiful and

~ ☾ ~

mysterious like the rings of Saturn. They drew me in immediately. Your nickname suits you perfectly."

She rested her head on his shoulder. He enjoyed her presence so much that he didn't even notice he was leading.

Soon everybody had found their match, and the dance floor was filled with newly formed couplets – all assembled to copulate and populate the new society with Perfect people – all of them perfect and desperately in love.

Stanford leaned in to whisper in Sarah's ear. "I'm indebted to the Policy."

She nestled her head further into his shoulder, comfortable.

Now, as he disembarked the fusion train and rushed up the front steps of the hospital, he felt the rings of Saturn bursting over like a dam.

~ ☾ ~

4.75 (THE ARRANGEMENT)

The same doctor he had seen the previous day met him in the emergency room.

"Mr. Samuels, come this way, please."

Stanford followed the doctor through a sterile corridor. There was a sense of urgency about the man. When they arrived at a waiting room, the doctor closed the door and instructed him to sit down. Stanford noticed another man in a lab coat sitting in one of the chairs.

"This must seem strange to you, Mr. Samuels," said the doctor. "I came as soon as I heard."

"I don't understand. Where is Sarah?"

"Please, Stanford," said the doctor. "We have very little time. I want you to listen to what Doctor Graves has to say. He's here from the Personal Associations Division."

Stanford looked at the man called Graves.

"Mr. Samuels, I wish we could meet under better conditions but since this is not the case, I will get straight to the point. We can make this less painful, but you must listen carefully to the options presented to you. This is a tragic thing, the most tragic thing imaginable, and I don't mean for a second to underestimate your loss, but we can bring her back. We mustn't lose time."

"My wife is dead?"

"Not exactly," said Graves. "She's brain dead in the sense that we legally consider her to be dead, yes, but there is enough neural activity that we can salvage her physical body and bring her back in a different way."

~ ☾ ~

Stanford looked between the two men, both leaning forward in their chairs, staring intently at him. He felt numb.

"What do you mean, in a different way? Are you saying you want to clone my wife? She didn't even approve of the reversal of the dog. What will I tell her when she comes home? 'Hi, honey, welcome back. Please try not to pee on the floor?'"

"Mr. Samuels, I must emphasize that I am not talking about cloning your wife. I am talking about revitalizing her. Think of her as a digitally enhanced photocopy of a person – a perfect replica without the genetic flaws inherent in most human beings. I am talking about a perfect synergy between mankind and technology. She will be the first of her kind. I urge you to consider the implications of this opportunity very seriously. Think about what this will mean to the Policy. You'll be a pioneer of the project, not to mention you'll have a chance to bear a child. We can't go forward without your consent."

"You want to make her a robot?"

"Not a robot," said Graves. "A super-organism."

The doctor cut in. "It needs to be done before the organs die, Stanford. I don't mean to sound cold, but if you want my professional opinion, I'd encourage you to take a chance. I know you and Sarah on a personal level, and I would not give you this advice if I didn't believe in it strongly. The Personal Associations Division is on to something very big that you can be a part of. If this seems rushed, it's because it is. We have to act now. We're asking you to take a leap of faith."

"But why Sarah?"

"For no other reason than the circumstances are right," said Graves. "The Personal Associations Division has not been ready to go forward with trials until now. Your wife is the first body to meet the criteria. She's a genetically acceptable vessel with the neurological

~ ☾ ~

activity that meets the standards for revitalization. As an added bonus, she's a Perfect. This is our first chance to go forward."

"I don't understand. How can you expect me to accept this?"

Graves seemed impatient. "We need to see if a reanimated woman can bear children to feed the Perfect colony. Regular eradication is working, but not at a rate that satisfies the Patron. We need to increase the population on the other side of the walls and we're looking at other, more efficient, ways of doing it. If we can reanimate a woman capable of bearing genetically cleansed offspring each and every time she gives birth, think of what we have accomplished, Mr. Samuels. Think of what it could mean for you and for the colony. If you give your consent, you will need to sign a confidentiality agreement that is very strictly enforced."

The doctor interjected, "Stanford, I know you learned to love Sarah through coupling. You loved her with all your heart, yet it was an artificial arrangement. After the initial coupling, did you see Sarah as anything other than a wife you loved and cherished? You had a future, and you can still have a future if you accept what we are offering. You can find love again, Stanford, but you need to trust us and give us the go ahead."

The information was coming fast; Stanford dropped his head in his hands and began to weep. His emotions were confused. He felt like he was losing control. "We wanted a child so badly."

"This arrangement can make you happy, Mr. Samuels," said Graves. "You can save yourself by giving the Patron a child. It's the next thing to a guarantee."

"Don't just do it for yourself, Stanford," said the doctor. "Do it for the Policy. It's not often a man has a chance to make his mark on the world and have love returned to him in the same stroke."

Stanford looked between both medical men. "Answer

~ ☾ ~

me one thing."

"What is it?" said the doctor.

"How did she die?"

The doctor's shoulders slumped. "She was struck down by a hover vehicle on her way to my office. I don't know the exact details. There's an investigation that you'll be made aware of, naturally."

"Why was she coming to your office?"

"She was worried about you, Stanford. She wanted to talk to me in person. I tried to convince her everything was fine, but she was insistent on seeing me. I felt I didn't have a choice, so I told her to come down to meet me. I'm so sorry this happened."

Stanford began to sob again. "Was the food list ready?"

"I'm sorry?"

"The food list ... she wanted to buy all new groceries that were safe for my condition. I made her upset because I told her it wouldn't be ready. All she wanted to do was take care of me."

"Don't blame yourself, Stanford. There's nothing you could have done to alter the past. It's the future you need to focus on."

"Was it ready?"

The doctor nodded. "The food list was being made up, yes."

Graves removed a sheet of paper from his pocket. "With your consent ..."

Stanford pictured his wife's face from the night of the coupling ball. She was beauty incarnate. He had loved her from the first moment he saw her, and he still loved her now. He imagined dipping her again, her hand touching the floor, and slowly leaning upwards to wrap her arms around his neck.

"I love you, Stanford Samuels ..." she said.

He was so happy when he looked into her perfect chestnut eyes. It was her eyes that brought them

~ ☾ ~

together.

Now he looked between the eyes of the doctors. If there was only one stipulation, it would be that his wife's name not be tainted.

"The new woman ... whoever ... whatever she is," he said, "she won't be called Sarah."

The men nodded in unison.

"Of course," said the doctor.

"Sign here," said Graves.

~ ☾ ~

5.0

The suns were out in full force, beating down on the beachgoers with both barrels. A young boy was attempting to build a castle in the sand, but sadly it was washed away by an incoming wave. Nearby, the boy's parents sat on a blanket eating sandwiches and enjoying cold drinks. The father wore long pants and shirtsleeves. He seemed uncomfortable under the glare of the twin suns.

The young boy had become so preoccupied watching his dog dig in the sand that he didn't notice the wave wash away the final remnants of his creation.

His mother called out, "Stanford, why don't you come have a sandwich and let me put some sunscreen on your back?"

When he looked back at his mother he could feel his sunglasses slipping down the bridge of his nose. He pushed them back up quickly, not wanting to reveal the flecks of copper in his irises that shimmered brightly in the natural sunlight. The genetic abnormality did not manifest in his carrier mother.

"Look, Mom," he said, pointing to the remains of his once mighty sandcastle.

"Yes, darling, you can build it back up after. Come now."

The boy got to his feet and walked towards the picnic blanket. He was covered from torso to toes with a light coating of sand.

"Brush off, Stanford," said his mother. "You'll soil the blanket."

~ ☾ ~

Stanford's father laughed. "You look like a sand monster."

Little Stanford furrowed his brow and curled his fingers like claws.

His parents laughed at his clowning around, and his mother helped him brush off before he sat on the blanket.

"Sit with your back to me. That's it." She squeezed a bottle of sunscreen into her hands and slathered it on his back. "They say the UV index is higher than ever."

His father grunted. "They are always stronger right before they die."

Stanford's mother patted him on the back when she was done. "Here, take this," she said, handing her son a sandwich. She looked at her husband. "They warned us for years about the suns. But what choice did they have?"

Her husband seemed distracted by the actions of the dog. "I suppose we deserve this then."

Stanford piped up as he munched on his sandwich. "What do we deserve, Dad?"

"Don't worry, honey," said his mother, "just finish your lunch."

Black dots invaded Stanford's vision when he tried to stare directly up at the suns. He looked back at his mother, waiting for her blurry image to clarify. "Mom?"

"Yes, dear?"

"Why aren't there two moons?"

"Where did you hear about moons?"

"Everybody knows about moons, Mom."

His mother chuckled at her son's precociousness. "Ultim doesn't have celestial satellites, Stanford."

"Celestial satellites?"

"We don't have moons."

"But we have two suns."

"Yes, dear, we have binary stars," explained his mother. "Suns and moons are independent bodies."

~ ☾ ~

Stanford tilted his head in thought. "Will they last forever?"

"Nothing lasts forever, darling."

"Will one last longer than the other?"

"There's no way of knowing. They are called White Dwarfs because they are old stars, but they could last several more lifetimes. Nobody knows for sure. But you have nothing to worry about."

His father grunted.

"Where will we go if the suns die, Mom?"

"There's nowhere else to go," said his father.

"Don't talk like that," said his mother, stabbing her husband with a hot glare.

Stanford thought for a moment. "Mom?"

"Yes?"

"What are binary stars?"

His mother laughed. "Maybe you'll grow up to be a scientist and you can explain it to me, honey. Now hurry and eat. We've got to go soon."

Stanford moaned. "What about my castle?"

His mother looked back at the spot where the castle used to be. The waves had not left a trace.

"Your castle is just another lost civilization, darling."

"Why can't we stay longer?"

"Your dad has to work, honey. We've had enough of the suns for one day."

"But Dad always has to work."

Both mother and child looked at father, as if he owed some sort of explanation, but he was too busy watching the dog to notice.

"One day you'll understand," said his mother. "But in the meantime, do what you're told."

The dog was deep inside a hole in the sand now.

Stanford's father got to his feet. "I better go see what the old boy is up to."

They watched him walk towards the hole with deliberate strides. When he got there he dropped to his

~ ☾ ~

knees and pulled the dog out by the scruff. He sat staring into the hole for a long moment before turning around and looking back at his wife.

Stanford's mother immediately got to her feet, sensing the disturbance in her husband's expression. "Wait here with the picnic basket. Do you hear me, Stanford?"

"Yes, Mom."

Stanford watched his mother walk to where his father was plunked in the sand. He saw his father's head drop forward on his chest. When his mother arrived she stared into the pit and raised her hand to her mouth to muffle a gasp.

Other beachgoers began to crowd around the hole. The beach was suddenly alive with commotion.

Despite his mother's orders, Stanford crossed the sand and pushed through the crowd to the edge of the hole to see what had caused such a ruckus. When he got there he had a clear view of the body of a dead woman lying twisted and awkward in the depths. The woman's long hair was pasted to the flesh on one side of her face, while the other side had been torn off to reveal a robot skull underneath.

Beachgoers scattered in panic, but Stanford stood at the edge of the hole without an ounce of fear. To him, the woman's face looked serene and peaceful, not the ugly remnants of a brutal ending. He wondered if she had found peace.

He could hear his mother demanding that he get away from the hole. Paying no attention, Stanford looked at his pet collie sitting nearby, wagging his tail like a metronome.

"You found her," he said to the dog. "You have a good sense of smell, old boy. Maybe one day you can be in the Militia like those helix-sniffing dogs. You're not mean enough though. You're a good old boy. I hope you stay with me forever."

~ ☾ ~

The dog looked at him from the other side of the hole, tilting its head and opening its mouth wide as if to yawn.

From out of the dog's mouth came the words, "Sarah ... Sarah ... Sarah."

~ ☾ ~

5.5

Stanford sat bolt upright. The comforter was bunched to one side, leaving only a thin sheet covering his sweaty torso. At the foot of the bed was the inert body of the robot aide.

The sleep arc was radiating so high he could hear the hum from the transmitter box on the nightstand.

He got out of bed as quickly as his sluggish body would allow and killed the signal on the black box. The room went dark, and he could hear the voice of the Patron on the radio coming all the way from the kitchen.

"The artificial environment is right on schedule, ready to protect our genetically superior civilization before the suns turn into neutron stars. It is up to each mutant to register for coupling in order to serve the Policy by offering an eradicated offspring to the Perfects. The Perfect colony is the lifeblood that will eventually feed Salus. Your place in the environment counts on your contribution, and your contribution is your obligation as a colonist. Our new society will exist not in sickness, but in health."

Stanford entered the kitchen and unplugged the radio by the cord, ensuring that it would no longer come on automatically in the morning. He sat heavily down at the table. His mind was flooded with hormones and it occurred to him that the arc might fry his brains if he set it any higher. He felt something wet on his toes and looked under the table to see the old boy licking his feet. The dog had developed some strange new habits since the second reversal.

~ ☾ ~

Stanford stood up and approached the cupboard, searching the shelves for dog food. He retrieved the bag of kibble and emptied the contents into the food dish before resuming his search for something that could pass as human breakfast.

There wasn't much to choose from as Sarah had emptied out all the food with high mineral content, not having a chance to replenish the old stock.

He glanced at the old boy eating from the food dish and for a moment considered getting down on his hands and knees and burying his face in the dish right along with him. The thought passed quickly.

As he exited through the archway, the front door buzzer blared through the foyer. He stood motionless before approaching the door and peered through the security hole.

On the other side was a man with a blue hat and a matching jacket. He recognized an ornate pin on the man's lapel. The initials engraved on the pin were *PAD*. Stanford knew it was the acronym for the Personal Associations Division.

He opened the door.

"I have a priority pod delivery for Stanford Samuels."

"I'm Samuels."

"I need verification."

The man pulled out an identification pen and flipped the cap. "Place your finger on the end, please."

Stanford did, feeling a prick at the tip of his finger. He waited while the man confirmed the genetic match.

"Okay, Mr. Samuels. I'll fetch your package."

Stanford watched the man return to the hover car and open the rear passenger door. A single shapely leg appeared from the back of the car, followed by another, and within seconds, Sarah was walking up the path towards him. She wore the same red dress she adorned the night of the coupling ball. Her hair and makeup were done to enhance all her best features. She smiled

~ ☾ ~

as she ascended the walkway.

When she reached the front door she said, "Aren't you going to invite me in?"

Stanford just stared like a fool.

"That's what I thought." She brushed past him and entered the foyer. "It's good to be home, Stanford."

"You look beautiful," he said, tentatively leaning to kiss her on the cheek. He caught a scent of the birthday perfume.

The dog scrambled into the foyer but stopped and back-pedaled when he saw Sarah.

"What's the matter, old boy?" she asked. "Don't you remember me?" Sarah chuckled and made her way through the front hallway into the kitchen, seeming quite at home. "Have you had breakfast yet?" she asked.

Stanford followed through the archway.

"No," he said. "The robot is still broken."

She looked back and smiled. "You don't need a robot, Stanford, you have me now."

He stood back, watching her open the fridge to peer inside.

"Not much here."

"I haven't gone grocery shopping yet," he said.

"This will do," she said, removing a package of eggs.

"Those should have been tossed out. I'm supposed to avoid eggs."

She stared at him with her perfect brown chestnut eyes. Her eyes were identical to his wife's.

"I want to cook for you, Stanford," she said with an overemphasized pout.

He couldn't resist the pout. "Okay," he said. "I can make an exception today."

She smiled and placed the carton on the counter. "Why don't you go freshen up while I get this started?"

"Okay."

Stanford turned to leave but paused when he reached the archway, glancing back at the figure in the red dress

~ ☾ ~

sweeping gracefully around the kitchen. For a brief moment he mistook the woman for his wife.

"I wish you hadn't worn that dress," he said quietly.

The woman turned. "What's that, dear?"

He hesitated. "What do I call you?" he finally asked.

"I'm Glenda," she said with a smile.

Stanford made his way down the hall towards the bedroom.

He made love to Glenda for the first time that night, submitting to his every desire – his every carnal need. The experience was cathartic. She was as close to human on the outside as was possible, but submissive as only an android could be. She was there to serve his every whim: in the kitchen, running errands, but most of all in the bedroom where they spent endless hours copulating for the sake of the Policy.

During their time together, Stanford turned his mind off and they lived every moment with a single vision to serve up an eradicated child to the Perfect colony. The only way he could cope with the arrangement was to refuse to listen to the inner voice that distinguished human beings from androids. The voice said: *This is not Sarah. She's gone.*

Each time he made love to Glenda he tried not to think of Sarah. He attempted to lose himself by fulfilling his physical fetishes and fantasies, but he always had a moment where he longed for his wife. He was losing the battle with the inner voice – not even the thought of producing a child to ensure his salvation in Salus was enough to quiet his subconscious chatter.

A few months after Glenda arrived, he made love to her more passionately than he had ever made love to Sarah, and when it was over he cried, overwhelmed by his own guilt.

"I'm so sorry, Sarah. I never meant for this to happen. I miss you so much …"

The voice was no longer on the inside.

~ ☾ ~

"I'm not Sarah …"

Glenda jumped out of bed and entered the en suite, slamming the door behind her.

Perhaps it was then Glenda came to realize that even though she was identical to Sarah in every physical way, she could never replace the woman he loved. It was Sarah's spirit he missed, which was something Glenda could never offer him.

So perhaps he should not have been surprised when he woke in his bed one morning and found Glenda gone.

~ ☾ ~

PART II: (GLENDA AND THE ELECTRIC FERN)

6.0

The explosions were beautiful and horrifying. Those who thought they were beautiful stared out the windows with a sense of awe, while those who were petrified clenched the armrests with white knuckles.

Stanford Samuels was neither horrified nor mesmerized. He was focused on the sound of atoms fusing beneath the floorboards as the train began its descent into the terminus. The sound was familiar and soothing. The train ground to a halt and signaled for disembarkation.

Outside, the loudspeakers were silent, the kiosks conspicuously abandoned. The platform was spotted with only a few mutant commuters; the fact was that it was dangerous to travel unless absolutely necessary.

Beyond the terminal the streets were in ruin, buckled by the weight of war machines, desolate with the exception of the physicals who looted the broken-down storefronts in search of supplies to take back with them. The physicals showed their ghastly mutations for the first time since the initial nuclear war – twisted features, extra appendages, seared flesh. They were truly ugly creatures, robbed of their previous identities.

Now that the Tech Terrorists had declared anarchy on the colonies, the physicals had returned from the outer boundaries with very little fear of capture. The police presence in the quadrants was stretched thin with the military focused on fending off the menace.

Each time a bomb hit somewhere in the colony, Stanford felt the shockwaves ripple under his feet. He pulled his solar visor down to the top of his sunglasses

~ ☾ ~

and made his way up the steps of the police station. It was one of the only buildings in the downtown core to remain intact. Standing at the front of the building he paused to take off his glasses so he could admire the structure for its resiliency. Amidst all the chaos, the center for maintaining order had remained untouched.

The lobby was much cooler than outside where the streets were super-conducted by smoldering rubble. He made a beeline through the booking section where a few repulsive looking physicals had been unlucky enough to be plucked off the street by one of the few patrolling cruisers, and then past a bank of offices towards the rear of the building. He stopped at the detective's office door, knocked, and waited until he was buzzed in.

Inside was a burly man in an oversized suit and a green tie with a clip bearing the insignia of his precinct. A nameplate on the desk read: "Detective William Briggs."

Briggs stared at Stanford with a look of utter exhaustion; dark, puffy circles afflicted both of his eyes. "What are you doing here, Saturn?"

"I told you not to call me that."

Stanford approached the desk, removing his visor and sunglasses. The copper rings around his pupils glimmered and spun with wild intensity.

"You look agitated, Stanford."

"I haven't heard from you for days."

"You haven't heard from me because there's nothing to say. Do you want me to call you every day to tell you I have nothing to tell you?"

"Where did she go?"

The detective exhaled impatiently. "We've been looking for Glenda in every nook and cranny in the mutant colony, Mr. Samuels. You'll notice I'm a little short on resources here, and if you care to look outside you'll also notice our priorities have shifted. I'm doing everything I can with what I've got. Unless she's gone

~ ☾ ~

underground, or slipped into the outer boundaries, we don't know where she is."

"I'm not talking about Glenda. I'm talking about Sarah."

The detective put his head in his hands. There was a long delay before he finally looked back at Stanford.

"We've been over this a hundred times, Stanford. Maybe all that copper in your eyes makes you see only what you want to see. Glenda is Sarah. Sarah is Glenda. They are the same bloody woman. I can't have this conversation with you right now. I don't have the patience."

The office rattled as a bomb dropped somewhere near the police station. Both men braced themselves until the shocks dissipated.

When things had settled the detective began to sort through a slush pile of paperwork on his desk.

"Our leads are exhausted. There's nothing more I can do at this time. I'll contact you if something changes. Maybe I'll contact you just to tell you that I have nothing to say. That should make you happy. Until then, maybe you should consider some counseling. Go see one of those electric ferns. I've heard they do wonders."

Stanford began to laugh manically. He back-pedaled a few feet from the desk and removed a glowing yellow handgun from the inside pocket of his jacket. The barrel was twisted like a corkscrew. He aimed the bizarre-looking weapon at the detective's forehead.

Inspector Briggs cackled. "Please shoot me, Stanford. I haven't had a day off in a year. I could use a long rest."

Stanford inserted the twisted barrel inside his own mouth and pulled the trigger, exploding grey matter mixed with bits of skull and hair all over the walls, covering the entire office in a red, soupy mess.

When his mangled head hit the ground, the rings of Saturn extinguished.

~ ☾ ~

6.3

"Good morning, Mr. Samuels."

The voice came from the shiny new robot aide that stood at the foot of the bed awaiting instruction.

"Your arc was too high, Mr. Samuels," said the Gen-3. "You must have suffered terrible dreams."

"To say the least," said Stanford.

A trickle of spittle ran down his chin and wet the pillow.

"The lower setting would significantly enhance your state of rest," said the robot.

"Have you considered that I set it that way on purpose?"

"Why would you do that, Mr. Samuels?"

"You wouldn't understand."

"Try me," said the robot.

Stanford sighed exaggeratedly as he struggled to prop himself up on the pillow. "I can't believe I'm having this conversation with you."

"I'm a high efficiency Gen-3 model with a broca chip. I've been programmed to carry on basic conversation."

"This isn't basic conversation. I miss my old robot. He minded his own business."

"Trust me, Mr. Samuels. I might surprise you. I'm really very intuitive to human nature. Tell me why you set the arc too high on purpose."

Stanford grinned. "I did it because I deserve to suffer in the morning."

The robot tilted its head to the side, imitating a look of curiosity. "Why do you think you deserve to suffer?"

~ ☾ ~

"I can't explain it to a machine. Not even to one with a broca chip."

The robot huffed. "As you wish, Mr. Samuels."

"Did you prepare breakfast?"

"Yes," said the robot. "Breakfast is served."

When the robot was gone, Stanford peeled the sweat-stained sheets away from his sticky body and moved slowly out of the bed one leg at a time. He went straight to the en suite, stepping into the condensation booth and sitting heavily on the meditation cushion. His body felt broken, his head thick and intoxicated. The transmitter had thrown his hormones so completely out of whack that he felt as if he were suffering the effects of a week-long alcoholic bender.

As the vapor enveloped him, parts of his dream came fluttering back, but the images were vague and disjointed. A yellow gun appeared to him through a curtain of steam before being sucked into the ether by the intake fan, terminated from his consciousness.

He sat with his head down until he heard the click of the door latch to indicate the cycle had ended.

When he stepped out, the eager tongue of the dog licked his feet. Stanford leaned over to give the old boy a good scratch. He had no idea what force it was that had bonded them since the day on the collie farm, but two reversals and thirty years later, here they were, together as always.

"It's just you and me, old boy."

Back in the bedroom he dressed in his finest formal attire the robot aide had selected the night before. The last time he had worn the grizzly suit jacket had been on the night of the coupling ball, which Sarah had later purchased from the rental company to commemorate their union. The fact was not lost on him, but before his mind could be dragged into a state of somber reminiscence, he was distracted by the newscast on the radio coming from the kitchen.

~ ☾ ~

*"After nearly thirty years of silence, the Tech
Terrorists are determined to show the world that they
are still a force to be reckoned with, announcing their
return in the most dramatic of fashions. For a second
straight day the colonies have been pelted with a
barrage of high-potency spray bombs, leaving the
quadrants in a state of pure destruction that hasn't
been seen since the last nuclear war. If the Tech
Terrorists have proven one thing with their
reprehensible actions, it's that they don't discriminate
between mutants and Perfects. Both sides of the wall
are fair game."*

Stanford entered the kitchen in his finest outfit. "I
don't like the radio on," he said.

The robot turned from the stove. "But consider what
is happening outside, Mr. Samuels."

"You consider too much," said Stanford. "I hope I
don't regret buying a unit with a broca chip."

The robot stared at him blankly.

"What are we having?" asked Stanford.

The robot was frying something on the stove that
created a large amount of smoke. "I guess the
condensation booth did little to lighten your mood, Mr.
Samuels."

"I don't need to hear it from you."

"I'm sorry, Mr. Samuels. I'll serve your breakfast at
the table."

Stanford looked closely at the robot and noticed the
smoke was not coming from the stove but rather from
the O-ring that connected the robot's head to its torso.

"We're having freeze-dried egg whites and special
potato hash," said the robot. "There's no copper in the
whites."

Stanford made his way to a window, cracking it open
to let out the smoke.

"I'm sorry, Mr. Samuels. I must have overcooked the
potatoes."

~ ☾ ~

Stanford stared out at the skyline. It was ominously quiet in the quadrant. It seemed almost surreal during breaks in the destruction. The silence was uncomfortable because the anticipation of violence was so much worse.

The Patron's voice was on the radio.

"To the terrorists who seek to destroy what we have worked so hard to build back up, I am speaking directly to you. How dare you sever the hand that feeds you. You have shown that your message is one of evil and destruction. There is no place in Salus for people like you. What awaits you instead is the merciless hammer of the Militia. You will be smoked out of the pits of Hell and hung like dogs in the central sector for the satisfaction of all mutants and Perfects alike. Our proud colonies are like a fledgling flower that pokes its face through the contaminated soil. We are resilient and will rise up again ...

"I assure you of only one thing: your death."

Stanford couldn't take it anymore. He turned off the radio before sitting at the table as the robot delivered breakfast.

"Let me cook more potatoes, Mr. Samuels. I'm worried I may have burned them."

"No need. These are fine. Will you replay the telegram from the Personal Associations Division?"

"Of course." The robot made the sound of rewinding and then emitted a voice that belonged to somebody else.

The voice said: "Mr. Samuels, you are invited to the Personal Associations Division to discuss the mishap with your bride-bot. Due to your involvement in the pilot project, the director insists on meeting you face to face. This opportunity is unprecedented and we ask that you treat it with the utmost respect. The meeting will be held on Tuesday. We will send a pod at noon. Please be prompt. End."

~ ☾ ~

There was a clicking sound as the message ended; the robot spoke with its own voice again. "Are you nervous, Mr. Samuels?"

"Why would I be?"

"The broadcasts are reporting extensive bombing downtown. It's dangerous to go outside."

"I appreciate your concern."

"Not only that, but it's not every day a person gets to meet the executive director of the Personal Associations Division. He serves the Patron directly."

"You mean it's not every day a mutant gets to meet with the director?"

"That's not what I said, Mr. Samuels. My broca chip does not allow for innuendo. Though what you say is true. Will you say hi to the director for me if the opportunity arises? I don't want you to go out of your way, of course – only if you can slip it in naturally."

Stanford approached the robot and patted him on the shoulder like an old friend. "No," he said, "but I'll talk to my parts guy about the black smoke that's coming out of your neck."

"What do you mean black smoke? Is it there now?" The robot was flustered and craned its head to see the smoke, like a dog chasing its own tail.

"Stop moving," said Stanford as he examined the O-ring. "No. It's not there now."

"What a thing to worry about," said the robot with a tone of panic.

"I know how you feel."

After quickly shoveling in the food, Stanford made his way to the foyer. "You're going to break my bank in the end," he said to the robot.

"I'm sorry, Mr. Samuels. The Gen-3 models have an unlimited warranty, but I would understand if you decided to trade me in on a less finicky unit. You don't need the trouble."

~ ☾ ~

Stanford patted the robot again. "You're staying right here with me, pal."

The dog joined them in the foyer, wagging its tail like a metronome.

Stanford opened the closet and selected his panda coat. It was his most formal-looking coat; the black and white fur was heavy and durable and had a long tail that flapped out behind when he walked. It was a perfect complement to the grizzly hair suit jacket.

"You two be good today," he said.

He couldn't help wonder which organism was less natural – the robot or the reversed dog.

This is my family, he thought.

Glenda had been a part of his family too, but she had abandoned them. He accepted the fact that he had not conceived a child with Glenda before she left, and that he would live out his remaining days in the mutant colony as a result, but he was happy to live it with his new family. There was honor in that – even if it meant freezing to death in permanent midnight.

He placed his sunglasses over his mutant eyes.

"Good luck," said the robot. "Be careful."

When he stepped onto the stoop he saw that the escort pod had already arrived. The hatch door opened. He looked at his watch. It was noon, on the dot.

~ ☾ ~

6.5 (THE GATEWAY)

Stanford experienced a feeling of déjà vu as he stared out the windows of the pod cruiser to witness the destruction in the downtown core of the mutant colony. The streets were barren with the exception of abandoned hover cars and various piles of rubble and garbage on the streets outside affected storefronts. In some cases, the rubble still smoldered with black nuclear smog. Entire strip malls had their windows blown out by the force of bombs. Shards of glass littered the streets. The devastation of war was everywhere. A shot ran up Stanford's spine as he recalled what had been here before and how quickly it had been leveled. He thought about how close the bombs had been to his home.

As the pod cruiser snaked its way through the broken region towards the giant walls, Stanford could see the gateway coming up quickly through the windshield. It was the main portal to the Perfect colony, presently guarded by a fortified steel fence. This was the passageway for the eradicated children, and he was gripped by paralysis as he realized he would soon be passing into the unknown territory. His lungs felt tight in his chest.

As the car advanced deliberately towards the portal, it became apparent the downtown core was not as abandoned as he had once thought. High above the gateway, perched on the tops of the walls, he could see the figures of the Militia's riflemen silhouetted by the twin suns, automatic weapons pointing in the direction of the cruiser. He was so engrossed in the scene before

~ ☾ ~

him that he was startled when the driver made a move to press a radio button on the console. The driver smiled at him through the rearview mirror and spoke into the radio.

"This is escort pod 2234, transporting mutant cargo, Stanford Samuels, by order of the director – requesting access to the gateway."

Now it was the driver's partner who glanced through the rearview mirror, examining him like an exotic animal at the zoo. Stanford looked away from the prying eyes.

Within moments, a voice crackled back through the radio, granting clearance. The gate rose off the ground, disappearing into a cavity inside the wall.

"Buckle up, Mr. Samuels," said the driver. "I know it's your first time."

Stanford tensed as the car moved slowly into the maw but once inside the darkness of the birth canal, he felt instant calm wash over him. There was no more anxiety. He felt no distinguishable emotion at all. It was what he imagined floating through space might feel like – a weightless sensation he had never experienced but could only dream of. He had no fear, only indifference. His lack of feeling confused him.

There was silence inside the car as they passed through the tunnel. The only light came from the controls that glowed on the dashboard, and when the pod breached the gateway, arriving on the other side, the first image to hit him was that of the familiar twin suns at their zenith, reigning brightly over the barren terrain.

He had spent a lifetime wondering what it would be like to cross over, speculating in his mind, debating with other mutants; now that he was through, he could only think how strange it was that the sky looked the same as where he had come from. He expected something different, more beautiful and awe-inspiring – for this

~ ☾ ~

was a perfect place. Yet, he had not landed on another planet or even arrived in another country, but simply crossed the walls to the opposite side.

He turned around to stare out the rear window. The walls, so massive up close, shrunk as the pod got farther away, and Stanford's mind struck with realization: *I've arrived in the Perfect colony.*

He looked around to take it all in. He felt a sudden urgency to soak in as much as he could before it was gone. The landscape was similar to what he had left. At first it was barren, gently rolling hills with very little vegetation, and as the cityscape appeared in the distance he saw evidence of war. Great clouds of smoke billowed above the skyscrapers like permanent black clouds. The war had a way of finding everyone, Perfects and mutants alike, and bringing all of them to their knees. He had a sudden thought: *The Tech Terrorists are winning. The dome will be breached and free for all to enter.*

He didn't know how to feel. The grip of the Policy was strong. He had spent his entire adult life trying to serve the Patron.

But the Policy has not served me.

Stanford noticed the driver looking at him through the rearview mirror.

"What did you expect," said the driver, "paradise?"

The officer in the forward passenger seat turned to face Stanford. He held up an injector pen. "I need you to hold still while I inject this into your neck," he said. "I don't want to sever your vein."

"What is it?" asked Stanford.

"It's an injection of I-132, commonly known as radioactive iodine. It emits small doses of radiation into your body that will gradually decay your organs. Given enough time, the radiation will cause you to go into shock and die. It's a most unpleasant death. However, if you return to the mutant colony in a timely fashion, you

~ ☾ ~

will be given the antidote and everything will be just fine and dandy. Consider it a security precaution for all mutants entering the Perfect colony – Patron's orders."

"But how many have entered before me?"

The driver chuckled. "You're the first."

Stanford looked between both officers carefully, noticing the pale complexion of their skin. Both men's pupils appeared abnormally small. Pupils that failed to dilate according to light conditions were a characteristic attributed to most androids. The irony was too much to ignore. He had finally crossed into the home of the genetically perfect population, and the first two individuals he met were androids.

He stared at the injector pen. "Do I have a choice?" he asked.

The driver snickered. "What makes you so special?"

Stanford turned his head to expose his jugular. He closed his eyes and felt the needle pierce his skin. When it was over the officer capped the needle and handed Stanford a surgical mask.

"Put this on."

"Why?"

"Just put it on, Mr. Samuels. You're in the Perfect colony now. We don't need you infecting us with your airborne germs."

Stanford stretched the elastic over his head and put the mask in place.

The driver was looking through the rearview mirror again. "Why do you wear those glasses, Mr. Samuels?"

"I'm sensitive to light."

"You'll be the only colonist on either side of the walls to be relieved when permanent midnight arrives."

Both officers shared a hearty laugh.

Stanford looked out the window as the pod approached the outskirts of the city. The road they had been traveling transformed into an expressway that connected to miles of arteries leading to various

~ ☾ ~

quadrants. The traffic seemed heavier here than in the
mutant colony as hover cars shot through the
interchanges at top speed. Clearly, synthetics were
filling out the population, giving the illusion of a
bustling metropolis in the colony that was otherwise flat
lining.

Ahead he could see a massive central tower in a
compound; on either side were smaller buildings that
pressed it like a sandwich. The compound was
enormous, surrounded by iron gates as tall and
foreboding as the walls that separated the colonies.

Unlike the void feeling he experienced when crossing
through the gateway, Stanford felt a very clear emotion
when he looked at the giant compound growing larger
in the windshield.

Stanford felt fear.

"Welcome to the Personal Associations Division,"
said the driver.

~ ☾ ~

7.0

"We'll be back in an hour," said the driver. "Remember the I-132. It really hurts after a while."

The driver laughed as the hatch closed and the jet engines ignited in the undercarriage.

Stanford stepped back to avoid getting scorched and watched the escort vehicle swoop away in a cloud of smoke. When it was gone he turned to see a woman in a charcoal colored suit jacket and matching knee-length skirt walking down the front steps of the Central Tower. Her jet-black hair was held in a tight bun by decorative sticks that bounced on her head as she walked quickly towards him. She looked sleek in black, with contrasting ruby red lipstick applied to her smiling lips.

"Welcome, Mr. Samuels. I'm Ilsa K." She extended her hand through the iron bars. "I'll be showing you to the viewing room."

The gate opened slowly on hydraulics.

"Did you have a pleasant trip, Mr. Samuels?"

"Yes, thank you."

"I'll assume you've never been to the Perfect colony before."

"No."

"Of course not." She smiled sheepishly. "I wish your first visit was at a more peaceful time, but I will try to make it as comfortable as possible for you under the circumstances. You are perfectly safe, I can assure you."

"Thank you. I appreciate your hospitality."

"Follow me. The director is expecting you."

As Ilsa K led him up the large marble walkway to the entrance, he thought about how nice her smile was, so

~ ☾ ~

pleasant and attractive, and the anxiety he felt before, though not completely gone, had diminished somewhat in her presence.

When they reached the top step of the Central Tower, Stanford looked down upon the expansive green-grass courtyard. From the vantage high above, the entire rectangular grounds were visible, completely enclosed by iron gates, with armed security guards patrolling the perimeter. He was taken aback by the thick blanket of protection, and for a moment his anxiety began to mount again.

"Shall we continue?" said Ilsa K.

Stanford turned back to his guide and returned her smile.

In order to gain access to the building, a camera on a serpentine neck extended from the top of the double doors and examined Ilsa K before turning its attention on Stanford.

"It's activated by motion sensor," she said. "It's extremely sensitive."

The neck swiveled to investigate every inch of his body, sniffing him like the flickering tongue of a snake, before retracting back into the hole above the door.

Ilsa K smiled as the doors unlatched to allow them entrance. "You've been cleared," she said.

They passed into a massive lobby with a seventy-foot ceiling painted entirely with a fresco of an idyllic forest teeming with wildlife and a babbling brook. The carpet was so plush beneath his feet it felt as though he was hovering just above the surface.

In every corner there were love seats accompanied by short tables holding old fashioned lamps adorned with flower printed shades; in the center of the room was an arrangement of friendly couches beneath an elaborate chandelier.

Stanford was captivated by the sight of such an incredibly elegant and welcoming lobby. Standing here,

~ ☾ ~

one would never know of the civil strife outside. He couldn't look at one side of the room for too long before having to quickly glance at the other. He considered taking off his glasses to take it all in with his naked eyes, but resisted the urge for fear of startling the girl.

"This is our executive wing," said Ilsa K, knocking him out of his reverie. "I can tell you're impressed by what you see."

He nodded, pivoting on his heels to take it all in. "I've never seen anything like it."

"You don't have anything like this in the mutant colony?"

"Not even close."

"After your meeting I can give you a tour of the compound, if you like. There's so much more I can show you."

"That's very kind of you."

He focused on his guide now. Ilsa K was a beautiful woman, her features almost doll-like with perfect proportions, strong cheekbones, and flawless skin. Her full red lips parted to reveal stark white teeth.

Sensing that she was being examined, she pivoted towards a long hallway leading away from the lobby. The hallway was laid with the same plush carpet that made it feel as though they were walking on air. He followed just a few paces behind, trying to absorb as much of the ambiance as possible.

Halfway down the hall was a display case nudged up against the left wall. He stopped to look inside and saw six ornate aluminum pendants backlit by soft white light. Each pendant was handcrafted with the image of a different animal: an eagle, a cobra, an owl, a lion, a moose, and a brown bear. He stared at each pendant with intense curiosity.

"They are cast from pure aluminum," said Ilsa K.

Her voice startled him. He was so mesmerized by the pendants he had almost forgotten she was there.

~ ☾ ~

"They symbolize animals that have already been introduced into the artificial environment – animals selected because they exhibit strength, courage, wisdom, freedom; all the core values the Patron holds in high esteem."

Stanford took his eyes off the pendants and glanced at Ilsa K. "Where are we right now?"

"This is the Central Tower, main lobby."

"I mean what is the street address?"

Ilsa K looked at him curiously. "We're on Idyllic Avenue. Why do you ask?"

He was silent for a moment. He felt a flutter in his chest. "It's not important," he said.

"There's a lot I can show you after your meeting. Follow me, please. We don't want to be late."

Nearing the elevators he noticed a short table with a lamp illuminating a bust of the Patron. There was a plaque at the base of the bust that said: *"Suns, Wind, Fire, Patron."*

Ilsa K stepped into the elevator. "We'll take it all the way to the penthouse," she said.

When the doors closed the elevator immediately began a fast ascent up the tower, causing Stanford a great deal of discomfort. Ilsa K sensed his distress.

"Lean against the wall," she said. "Hold onto the rail. It will be over in a moment. There we are."

The elevator came to a sudden halt and the doors opened upon another elegant hallway that terminated at a set of steel doors on the far end. Stanford took a moment to collect himself before joining her in the hallway.

"That's our viewing room, Mr. Samuels. The director will meet you there momentarily."

As they neared the doors at the end, she stopped him with her hand. Her voice took on a conspiratorial tone now.

"I'm not supposed to say so, but if you look out the

~ ☾ ~

north window, you can see the dome of Salus way off in the distance. Construction is nearly complete. I'll leave you here. Good luck, Mr. Samuels. Perhaps I'll see you later."

"Thank you, Ilsa K."

"It was my pleasure, Mr. Samuels."

She turned on her heel and walked briskly back down the hall just as the steel doors of the viewing room began to open on their own. Stanford took a final glance towards Ilsa K, but she had already disappeared into the elevator.

Stepping into the viewing room, he could see one hundred-eighty degrees of curved windows displaying a panoramic view of the colonies from miles above. There wasn't a single item of furniture anywhere in the room to impede the view. Every surface, from the floor to the ceiling, had been plated with polished titanium, creating a lightshow effect as the rays of the twin suns entered through the windows and refracted off the surfaces at all different angles.

Stanford stepped towards the curved window and looked out at the entire north sector of the Perfect colony, and when he glanced far to the left he could see the wall segregating the mutants, so small at this distance it hardly resembled the intimidating structure he knew it was.

It was a magnificent view from way up high and he couldn't help but feel a moment of bliss. This was freedom, like a bird escaping from its cage after years in captivity, and now flapping its wings across the sky, riding an air current to a better place.

He remembered what Ilsa K had said and looked straight ahead through the north window, scanning the colony all the way to the distant edge that separated the northern sector from the outer boundaries, but he did not detect Salus. Certainly a dome large enough to house the artificial environment would be plain to the

~ ☾ ~

naked eye. Had she been mistaken about which window to look out?

A door opened from the rear, and he turned around to see a well groomed man in a tuxedo approaching very quickly. The man stopped within inches of him, standing perfectly erect.

"Mr. Samuels, you are here to discuss the Glenda project. Matters concerning the whereabouts of Glenda are for the police, not for the director. You will only hear this once. Do you understand?"

"Yes."

With that, the man turned and disappeared through the rear door as quickly as he had arrived.

Stanford watched the door a moment longer, thinking about what an oddity the man's presence had been, before advancing towards the north window to resume his search for Salus. He felt like a mischievous child looking at something forbidden.

He scanned the eastern sector now, thinking perhaps Ilsa K had been confused about the location of the dome. An explosion rose up in a plume of brilliant crimson that filled the viewing room and refracted off the metallic surfaces, splitting into hues of red and orange and yellow. As the colors lost intensity and slowly faded out, Stanford sensed he was not alone. He turned to see a silhouette of a man watching him from a dark corner, his figure cloaked entirely in a shadow that took residence against the far wall. He wondered how long the man had been there.

After a moment the man said, "You are Mr. Samuels?"

Stanford instinctively raised his hand to remove the surgical mask.

"Leave it on. And stay where you are."

Stanford froze and slowly lowered his hand.

"You are the man they call Saturn?"

"Yes."

~ ☾ ~

Even from a distance, Stanford could hear the man wheeze.

"You are the one with Wilson's disease, yes? You have eyes like none other."

"So I've been told."

"What is the purpose of such a strange genetic anomaly, Mr. Samuels?"

"What do you mean?"

"Does it offer you advantages? Can you see in the dark? Can you see my face through the shadows?"

"No."

"Then this strange disease only brings you pain and suffering. It makes you different for no good reason. How can that be, Mr. Samuels? How can God be so heartless?"

"I can't answer that."

The man chuckled. "I don't mean to enter into some kind of theological debate. Do you know who I am, Mr. Samuels?"

"The guide told me you were the director."

"Yes, she is a lovely woman, isn't she?"

"She was very kind."

"Indeed. We are lucky to have Ilsa K on staff. And she is right about what she told you. Did she also tell you why I invited you here?"

"I have an idea."

"Well good, we can get right to it. You well know, as director of the Glenda project, I'm accountable for the failure of Glenda to reproduce, and also for her abandonment of you, Mr. Samuels. That was not supposed to happen. You tried your best, and we appreciate that. I've read the activity logs; your stamina in the bedroom is impressive."

Stanford could see the man bring something up to his mouth that sounded like a ventilator.

After replacing the device in his pocket the director said, "You wonder if I have asthma? You wonder how

~ ☾ ~

the executive director of the Personal Associations Division could have a disease of the lungs. Is that what you are wondering?"

Stanford hesitated. "I hadn't thought of it."

"Sure you thought of it, Mr. Samuels. There's no harm in curiosity. In fact, curiosity is what drives us here at the Personal Associations Division. It's what propels our experiments forward. It's a beautiful thing, curiosity. It's a thing of science. You can admit that just now you wondered how a man who works immediately beneath the Patron, in a colony where diseases are strictly forbidden, could possibly bear a mutant gene. Is that what you are wondering, Mr. Samuels?"

Stanford heard the man wheeze.

"The answer, Stanford, is my lungs get irritated from all the dust floating in the air. It's exacerbated by the unusual conditions outside. The only thing that alleviates my cough is an inhaler designed for asthmatics. Would you do me a favor? Would you come closer, please, and uncover your face? I'm ready to see you now."

Stanford complied.

"Your eyes are beautiful in this low light," said the director. "They shimmer like the night sky. Mutation is not always ugly, is it?"

Another mushroom cloud illuminated the northeast window and sparkled throughout the viewing room.

The director sighed. "And war is not always ugly, either, Mr. Samuels. Just look out at that spectacular fire in the sky. What a shame something so pleasing to the eye brings with it so much suffering. My heart goes out to your people, too, by the way. This is all so unfortunate and unnecessary."

Stanford could hear the man struggling to breathe.

"Mr. Samuels, would you be so kind as to accompany me to my personal therapy room? I'm finding the air rather stuffy in here."

~ ☾ ~

"Certainly."

"Grand. Follow me, please."

Stanford followed the director through the rear door.

Soon they were in an anteroom filled with loveseats and dim lighting. The soothing sound of running water was piped in from above. For the first time Stanford could see the director's face. He was a perfectly attractive gentleman, middle-aged, with a square jaw and high forehead, and slightly flushed skin. He sat down on a plush leather sofa and loosened his tie, gesturing for Stanford to sit in any of the available loveseats.

"I come in here when I need to decompress," said the director. "I find it soothing, don't you?"

"Yes, it's very comfortable."

"It's my therapy room. Everything about it pacifies me. Do you hear the sound of running water?"

"Yes."

"It comes directly from a wireless microphone located all the way at the base of a waterfall in the artificial environment. Water therapy is said to be outmatched in its ability to calm the body by only one thing. Do you know what that one thing is?"

"No."

"Mr. Samuels, have you ever seen an electric fern?"

Stanford was silent.

"They have a calming influence that is uncanny, more efficient than any naturally occurring substance on Ultim. There is one over there in the display case if you'd like to see it. It's behind the curtain."

The director sensed his hesitation.

"Go take a look," said the director. "It's wonderful."

Stanford's previous encounter with an electric fern made him reluctant, but he knew the director wouldn't be satisfied unless he could show off his possession. He walked towards the curtain and pulled it aside to reveal the display case. Inside, the fern swayed like a seductive

~ ☾ ~

woman, matching the rhythm of the piped in waterfall.

The director waited for Stanford to get a good look. "What do you think, Mr. Samuels?"

Stanford watched the little bubbles of green energy rising off the leaves and popping against the inside of the glass. "It's quite something."

"Open the case, Mr. Samuels. Feel the fronds with your bare hand. You have to physically connect with the fern to get the full effect. It's a sensation like no other. Go ahead."

Stanford opened the glass and reached tentatively towards the plant. The leaves recoiled.

The director laughed. "She's shy. Let her get used to you. Try not to seem nervous or she will sense it. Imagine yourself meeting a stranger for the first time. There is a moment of trepidation before the ice is broken. That's what's happening now."

Stanford offered his hand to the plant again. This time a broad, feathery leaf came out to investigate. The frond brushed against his hand, exploring his wrist with great curiosity and then wrapped around his arm all the way to the elbow. The leaf was silky smooth and charged with static that prickled Stanford's skin. The sensation was entirely pleasant.

"She seems to have taken a shine to you, Mr. Samuels. What do you see?"

Suddenly Stanford was transported to a new place. One minute he was in the therapy room, the next he was here. The transition was instantaneous.

He could see a waterfall in the clearing of a thick tropical forest. He approached cautiously through the tangled bank, careful with his footfalls. As he got closer there was a beautiful woman bathing in the frothy cascade. She was waist-deep in the brilliant green pool, her long brown hair covering the mounds of her breasts. She smiled when she saw Stanford standing at the edge.

"I was wondering when you'd come," she said.

~ ☾ ~

"I didn't know where you went."

"I'm glad you came." She beckoned to him. "Come in with me. The water feels wonderful."

"I don't have a change of clothes."

Stanford stepped forward, eying the nape of her neck, glancing all the way down to her perfectly tear-shaped navel.

She waded towards him. Climbing out of the water, she revealed the beautiful parts that had been hidden. She walked up to him, gently touching his face with her wet palm.

"Your eyes are better," she said. "They are as green and calm as the water."

"The fern cured me."

"I'm so glad," she said. Then she took his hand. "Come, I want to show you something."

She led Stanford along an overgrown path through the dense underbrush. The trees were massive, stretching a hundred meters into the sky, their canopies creating a state of permanent twilight on the ground.

When they reached a clearing the naked woman stepped off the path and knelt behind a giant, old log. She gestured for Stanford to kneel next to her and pointed into the clearing about thirty yards ahead where a doe and its baby were indulging on the vegetation.

"Aren't they beautiful?" she said.

He knelt down next to her and nodded. He loved to see her smile.

"They come back every day at this time. I like to watch them. Sometimes the buck will come too and they will eat together like a family at the dinner table." She took his hand. "It's so nice to see you, Stanford. I miss our family. I'm glad I could share this with you."

He felt a wave of emotion. He knew she felt it too.

Tears welled in her perfect chestnut eyes.

Then she looked forward again, pointing high up into

~ ☾ ~

the canopy at a black spotted bird with orange and
yellow patterns on its tiny head. "It's a Gilded Flicker,"
she said. "I looked it up in my bird book."

"You found the book?"

"Yes. It was in my dresser drawer, right where I left
it."

She brushed away the tears that streaked out of
Stanford's emerald green eyes.

"Why did you leave me?" he asked.

"I'll always be with you," she said, and she took
both of his hands in hers and pulled him into an
embrace.

They held each other tightly for a long while.

"I don't want to let you go, Sarah," he said, voice
quivering. "I love you."

"I love you, too, Stanford Samuels. I always will."

She held him a moment longer but then it was time
to go. She stood up, leading him back down the
overgrown path the way they had come. When they
pushed through to the other side, Stanford was back in
the therapy room.

The fern unwound from his arm and returned to its
home in the display case. The plant went completely
dormant; its green aura faded and it appeared like any
other potted plant. Stanford had been released from its
power.

The director's voice came from behind. "How do you
feel, Mr. Samuels?"

Stanford turned slowly to face him. "I don't know. I
feel calm, but slightly scattered. It's a strange
sensation."

"I know exactly what you mean. It's like the fern
takes your greatest fears and simply absorbs them into
its leaves. The first time is a mixed bag because your
body rejects it like it would any foreign presence. Each
time gets a little better. I can't live without it now. "

Stanford made his way slowly back to the loveseat,

~ ☾ ~

still feeling dazed from the vision. He needed to sit down.

"Let me get you a drink to perk you up, Stanford."

The director pressed an intercom button on the armrest. "Send in Alice with a drink for our guest."

After he had spoken the command, he sat back and looked directly at Stanford. "I've used enough of your time, Mr. Samuels. Let's get to it then. I want you to know our corporation is forever indebted to you for being part of the pilot project. Your suffering is not in vain. Our technicians have already taken the necessary steps to fix the flaws inherent in the Glenda unit. We'd like you to be part of the next stage of the process. Do you follow me, Mr. Samuels?"

The director was interrupted by a woman with a sleek body in a tight fitting red dress. She entered the therapy room with a drink tray.

"Mr. Samuels," said the director. "It is my honor to introduce you to the Alice-2. She is our newest model, the next step up from the Glenda unit on the evolutionary ladder, so to speak."

Stanford accepted the drink. He couldn't take his eyes off the dress.

The woman looked at him and smiled.

"We are so proud of Alice," said the director.

The Alice unit's cheeks flushed as she set down the tray.

"As you can see, Mr. Samuels, her limbic system is fully functional. Greet our guest, Alice."

"Sorry. How rude of me." She extended her hand. "It's a pleasure to meet you, Mr. Samuels."

"Likewise."

Her hand was warm; he could feel a pulse beating in her wrist.

"Electron accelerators have been implanted in her spinal column to replicate the human nervous system. Alice's reflex activity is controlled by electrons rather

~ ☾ ~

than the outdated gearboxes of the older models. The result is a significant upgrade, as you can see for yourself. She can complete the most complex arithmetic problems without effort. You won't have a problem with your taxes, I can assure you."

Alice smiled modestly.

"I can see you are impressed, Mr. Samuels. Alice's cognitive functioning exceeds the highest IQ scores ever recorded. We've even installed an automatic shutdown feature in the central nervous chip that is voice-activated by keywords programmed into her CPU. It's literally impossible for her to defy her programming. Allow me to demonstrate."

Alice smiled at Stanford again and then looked at the director in anticipation of the command. "What will you have me do, boss?"

"Alice, I want you to misbehave for our guest."

"But I don't know how to misbehave, boss."

Her voice was silky smooth and heartbreakingly innocent.

"Of course you don't, dear."

The director addressed Stanford again. "We have preprogrammed this particular unit to shut down upon hearing the command 'roll over.' For demonstration purposes, the sound and pitch of my voice was previously encrypted in her central nervous chip. The mechanism can only be activated when I speak the command directly to the Alice unit. Observe the keyword command."

The director spoke to the android clearly now, enunciating every syllable, holding her gaze. "I-want-you-to-mis-be-have-now."

Alice's face contorted. "But I don't know how to misbehave." Her lower lip quivered.

The director persisted. "Misbehave now!"

"I can't!"

Tears began to streak down the android's cheeks.

~ ☾ ~

"Note the activation of the advanced limbic system, Stanford. Now listen for the keyword command. Roll over!" he shouted. "Roll over at once!"

Alice's eyelids slammed shut and her head fell forward on her chest. She was inert now, peaceful looking. Even the breathing mechanism had stopped.

The director harrumphed. "You see? This unit is foolproof. It's the most advanced bride-bot ever created by the Personal Associations Division. This is what I'm offering you. I'd like you to continue to be a part of the project, Mr. Samuels."

"What do you mean?"

"Take the Alice-2. Use her as your servant around the house, a slave if you will. Treat her like you would any other subservient android. I'm not asking that you accept her like the Glenda bot. I know the depth of the pain you have suffered. Consider this more like a casual relationship."

"I already have a robot aide."

The director stood up. "Come with me."

Stanford followed the man back into the viewing room. They stood before the windows, staring out at the panoramic view of the Perfect colony in silence, savoring a moment of peace. A massive explosion rose up and scorched the sky.

"Destruction is sometimes beautiful, just like mutation is sometimes beautiful," said the director. He looked at Stanford now. "Creation is the most beautiful of all. I want you to make a child, Mr. Samuels. The goal of the project remains to serve the Policy. We must yield genetically eradicated children as fast as we can, by any means necessary. If the Alice-2 can successfully correct a mutant gene as rare and as mysterious as the one you carry, think of the possibilities. Think of what it could mean for the future of Salus. We are so close, Stanford. The Alice-2 may be our breakthrough. You can be a part of that."

~ ☾ ~

Stanford stared at the rising plume over the northern sector. "And why would I do that? Why would I continue to live like a guinea pig?"

The director smiled. "Why else? So you don't freeze to death when the suns burn out."

"Where does that leave us?" asked Stanford.

"Us?"

"The mutants. You're essentially taking our jobs away."

"This isn't a union, Mr. Samuels. This is private enterprise. If the mutants can't get the job done at the rate it needs to get done, then they will be replaced by those who can. Besides, there are lots of jobs to go around. I wouldn't worry too much about the mutants. Just worry about what you can do for the Policy."

Stanford continued to stare forward out the window.

The director made a sudden pivot. "Now, if you'll excuse me, I have other business. Consider it, Mr. Samuels. I'll give you a few days to mull it over. If you decide to accept the offer, I'll send Alice to your house on the priority pod. If I was in your position, I'd realize there are far worse fates than being asked to copulate with a beautiful woman in order to save yourself and serve your colony. Your escort is waiting. Put your mask back on."

Stanford watched the man disappear into shadows and exit through the rear door, wheezing the entire way out.

~ ☾ ~

7.75

Ilsa K was standing in the hallway outside the doors of the viewing room. She flashed her warm smile when Stanford came out. He fumbled in his breast pocket for his glasses and quickly placed them over his eyes.

Ilsa K's smile faltered for an instant before broadening once again. "How did it go?"

"It went fine," he said.

They walked side by side down the hall and stepped into the waiting elevator. When the door closed Ilsa K glanced over at him.

"Do you always cover your face?"

"I don't normally wear a mask, but I always wear the sunglasses."

"Oh." She paused for a moment.

He could sense she had more questions.

"Do you have time for a tour?" she asked.

"The escort pod is waiting to take me back to the mutant colony."

Ilsa K looked disappointed.

When the elevator doors opened, they stepped into the hallway that led back to the lobby.

"Maybe another time," she said.

He nodded, wondering how she could possibly think there would be another time.

When they got to the lobby Ilsa K removed a business card from her pocket. "Take this. It has my number. If you're ever back this way, I'd be happy to show you around."

~ ☾ ~

He looked at her sweet face and was sorry he'd never see her again.

"Thank you, Ilsa K."

"Have a safe trip back, Mr. Samuels."

With that, she turned and walked back down the hall.

~ ☾ ~

8.0 (TECH TERRORIST)

"Leave your mask on till we get back to the gateway," said the driver.

Stanford looked silently out the rear window as the cruiser surfed through a web of interchanges on the way to the city limits. The buildings in the downtown core were nothing more than streaks across the windows; the structures had no significance at all. The effort of processing the surroundings, as small as it was, was a wasted effort. It was the last time he would be here.

Instead he closed his eyes and thought about Ilsa K. She was worth the effort, he thought, but she was gone too. He'd never have another chance to experience her smile, to stand with her in an awe-inspiring lobby and be so acutely aware of her presence.

It was a shame. She had shown kindness and treated him as an equal, even though it would have been easier for her to look at him as a mutant. She could have been cold to him. He would have understood it. In a strange way, it would have been better had she rejected him. Then he wouldn't be thinking about her at this very moment. He felt a deep sorrow knowing Ilsa K would live on the other side of the walls, and they would go about their lives without contact, like perfect strangers, and eventually their memories of each other would fade. Ilsa K was like the rush of buildings through the windows of the cruiser. She was there and then gone. He'd never know these buildings. He'd never know Ilsa K.

When he opened his eyes he saw the cruiser had taken a wide berth around an overturned passenger

~ ☾ ~

vehicle, its front end crumpled to the forward thrusters, while emergency responders attempted to pry open the mangled hatches.

The cruiser stopped. The driver rolled down the side window to address an emergency responder.

"You've got a situation here," said the driver.

The emergency responder leaned to look inside the cruiser. His voice was muffled behind a gas mask. "What we've got is a full-blown circus," he said. "The whole colony is on its way to the hanging square. There are an estimated sixty thousand hover vehicles traveling to the city center at the same time. I've seen three pile-ups come in on the videophone in the past twelve minutes alone."

"You've certainly got your hands full," said the driver. "Sorry we can't help. We have a transport."

The responder turned the big black insect eyes of his mask towards the back seat to get a look at Stanford. "Where are you taking him?"

"We're delivering him back to the mutant colony where he belongs."

"It will be slow going," said the responder. "With all the traffic, people have abandoned their vehicles and taken to foot; they're crossing the road at will. We've radioed in for some extra help, but it's congested just about everywhere. We're undermanned."

"It's understandable," said the driver. "Good luck out there."

The emergency responder backed away from the escort pod. "Drive safely," he said.

As the cruiser advanced the driver's partner turned to address Stanford. "I bet you're wondering what's going on. They caught one of the Tech Terrorists about an hour ago," he said. "It's all over the news. Apparently he was hiding on your side of the wall. They're bringing him back to hang. The Patron wants to make an example out of him. While you're going that way, he's

~ ☾ ~

coming back this way. Like two ships passing in the night."

The officer grinned and faced forward in his seat.

Stanford looked back out the window, trying to look stoic despite the pang he felt in his gut.

What does this mean? What will become of the man? Is the rumor true that they are all physicals?

It didn't take long for the procession of Perfects to appear up ahead. Thousands of genetically superior colonists flooded across the road on their way to the hanging square at the center of town.

Watching the procession, it occurred to Stanford this was the first time he had witnessed so many Perfects in one place, and he couldn't help but notice they had the perfect amount of bloodlust.

Soon the cruiser was forced to stop. The crowd was so thick it was impossible to move forward or back.

The officer in the passenger seat glanced over at the driver. "I guess we wait it out."

The driver was clearly agitated. "Where's the extra help?"

"I don't see any uniforms."

"We've got to clear the road," said the driver. "I'm not putting in overtime. Not for a mutant. This is a ridiculous assignment. Wait here."

The driver exited the vehicle and began waving his hands at the crowd in an attempt to create a gap to drive the car through, but it didn't take long for him to be swallowed up in their midst. The vehicle began to rock gently back and forth as the wave of Perfects edged by. Some gawked through the windows. Stanford felt a rush of anxiety. The energy outside the car was supercharged.

The officer in the passenger seat looked back at Stanford. "I'll be right back," he said. "Remember the I-132. Don't be stupid."

The second officer got out of the vehicle and tried to

~ ☾ ~

halt the crowd, just as his partner had done moments earlier. Stanford could hear him yelling at the crowd about obstructing a police operation, but the Perfects pushed by him like he wasn't there. The only justice at this moment, it seemed, was at the hanging square.

Stanford glanced at the door handle, noticing the preoccupied officers had inadvertently left the locking mechanism open in their haste. He thought about the life awaiting him on the other side of the walls. He pictured Sarah at the coupling ball, in the red dress he loved so much, leading him by the hand to the dance floor. His mutant eyes met her perfect brown chestnuts, and he could hear her voice: *I love you, Stanford Samuels.*

Stanford put his head in his palms and sobbed. Sadness and fear shot through his body like powerful adrenaline.

What more is there for me? What more can this life take from me? The director asked why God would give me mutant eyes. Is there a god? Would a god create a colony of mutants? Why would a god give so much power to a man like the Patron?

Thinking of Ilsa K, he reached into his breast pocket and removed the business card. Turning it between his trembling fingertips he saw the backside of the card bore a rough hand-sketched image of a distant planet in the Milky Way galaxy called Saturn; the rings shaded dark for emphasis.

He stared at the sketch for a moment, thinking about how the rings cast a mysterious and foreboding shadow over an otherwise unremarkable and uninhabitable ball of gas. He wondered about the significance of the rings, whether the artist emphasized them to make a point or for no reason at all. Sometimes there was no point. It was easy to look too hard for answers.

He turned the card over, seeing the phone number, before putting it back in his pocket and closing his eyes.

~ ☾ ~

Now he could see Ilsa K in his mind. She was so beautiful. He didn't want to live on the other side of the walls and allow her memory to fade.

He looked through the windshield and scanned the mob for the officers, but they were nowhere to be seen. He moved quickly, removing the surgical mask from his face and depositing it on the floor of the cruiser. In an instant he was outside. He took a moment to scan the mob again. If the officers were there, he could not see them.

If I hide my eyes, I can blend in with these people for as long as my organs can withstand the radiation. How long do I have? They didn't tell me. I will die if I stay here, but I can't go back to the mutant colony. I've lost too much there. Sarah is gone and every day feels like death without her. Old boy can take care of himself. Besides, he's taken care of me too long; he'll finally be free of my burden. I have no one else.

He thought about the old man with haemochromatosis; the man was the closest person Stanford had to a friend.

I hope he'll be okay. I will miss our lunches together. But he's been alone most of his life anyway. He will get by just fine. My life in the mutant colony is irrelevant, and that's worse than anything I can experience here. Reece was right: There is nothing worse than dying in the cold all alone. There is hope here. I need to find Ilsa K.

Before he could talk himself out of it, Stanford fell in line with the procession of Perfects. He blended in perfectly.

~ ☾ ~

8.3

The mass of bodies swelled like a single entity. Right at the vortex of the mob, Stanford kept his head bent to the ground, watching his feet to keep pace with the Perfects who engulfed him. As the procession began to slow, Stanford glanced up, seeing two solid stone pillars standing tall in the midst of a main intersection. The columns were on either side of the gallows, carved like totems depicting the heads of the animals he had seen on the aluminum pendants. At the top of each column was the bust of the Patron. They had arrived at the hanging square.

The crowd roared as the executioner stepped onto the elevated platform. Behind the cloaked man, a giant black video screen acted as a backdrop. The executioner raised his hand, and the crowd fell deathly silent at once.

"For committing abominable offences against the colonies, the Patron has ordered this man to hang until he gasps his last breath and every ounce of life trickles from his body and wets the contaminated ground under his feet. What the Patron wants, the Patron gets."

The crowd roared like hungry savages as the Tech Terrorist was escorted up the stairs to the platform.

Stanford cheered too. "Serve the Policy," he shouted along with them. "Serve the Policy!"

The words seemed to escape his lips by accident; he was totally caught up in the vibe of the crowd.

The terrorist was pulled along the platform by a chain attached to his neck. He walked with an obvious limp. He was pathetic – a dirty physical with a club foot.

~ ☾ ~

When the hangman placed the dark hood over the man's head he spoke again.

"This mutant has caused grievous sins against humanity. His actions, though not orchestrated by him alone, will be judged as his own when he arrives in the kingdom beyond the infinite. Our concern is not what happens to him there, but what happens to him now. It has been pronounced by the Patron: Today is Judgment Day!"

The crowd's hankering for blood was palpable.

Suddenly the video screen came alive with an image of the Patron. A great chiseled visage with piercing dark eyes looked upon the audience like a father upon his legions of children.

"Welcome citizens of the Perfect colony. We are gathered today to celebrate our latest victory over the savage menace, the Tech Terrorists. The atrocities committed against our colonies by these rogues are beyond comprehension and a threat against all that we hold dear. Our vision of populating Salus with a super race will not be compromised by militants who seek to cause havoc through war and chaos. The Policy is bigger than any uprising, and we will prove the power of our collective spirit by hunting down the insurgents and crushing them without mercy. Today we have an opportunity to show the Tech Terrorists who we are and to avenge what they have taken. The Policy remains strong. To all of you Perfect people before me, and to the families who have adopted, as well as those Eradicators on the other side of the walls who carry out our mission, I want to thank you for being the best colonists you can be. Your place in the artificial environment has been cemented. You have made all of us proud. Our new society will exist not in sickness but in health.

"Now turn the beast to face me and remove the hood."

~ ☾ ~

The executioner turned the man with a force strong enough to buckle the offender's knees. He pulled the man viciously to his feet by the chain around his neck, ripping the hood from his head to reveal the burdened features beneath.

"Let my face be the last thing you see before you exhale your final breath on Ultim. You will not achieve the salvation of Salus. As the father of the colonial world, I hereby sentence you to death by hanging."

Under the deafening chorus of encouragement, the hangman detached the chain and placed the noose around the terrorist's neck. Tears streaked down the man's mottled face. He closed his eyes.

"Today is Judgment Day!" cried the hangman. "Serve the Policy!"

The crowd chanted the chorus in unison: "Serve the Policy, serve the Policy ..."

Stanford repeated it too. *Serve the Policy. Serve the Policy!*

The fall was quick and startling. The rope snapped violently but it did not kill the man. What followed was a brutal display of torture. A man hanging from the end of a rope around his neck, choking off his oxygen supply, kicking and writhing his legs at the empty air, begging for mercy without a voice, lips blue and swollen, eyes bulging like a dead fish for what seemed like eternity, yet was less than one minute. The man gasped his last suffocating breath, horrified and unable to find peace – legs shaking out the last remnants of vitality. A life was snatched away forever.

The video screen went black. The message was delivered.

Stanford clutched his stomach as he slipped through the maze of chanting Perfects, away from the hanging square. The tall buildings in the downtown core that had previously seemed so insignificant, now served the invaluable purpose of shielding him from the eyes of the

~ ☾ ~

officers who would most certainly come looking for him.

He felt sick after what he witnessed. Seeing a man die the way he had – at such close proximity – made Stanford realize that he didn't share the Perfects' enthusiasm.

As he searched for refuge a surge of pain pierced his stomach. The radioactive implant was beginning to poison him; the death he had just witnessed would seem like a mercy killing compared to what was in store for him.

~ ☾ ~

8.5

Mindful to stay off the main thoroughfares, Stanford found a telecommunications booth on an empty walkway several blocks from the hanging square. He could still hear the hum of the crowd in the distance. He knew it was only a matter of time before the streets became crowded with satisfied Perfects, returning home like fat cats after a live meal.

Stepping into the booth he removed the business card from his pocket and stared at the sketch of Saturn for a moment before dialing the videophone.

Ilsa K's face came on-screen.

"Oh, hello, Mr. Samuels."

Her face instantly turned from recognition to confusion.

"What are you doing? Where are you?"

Stanford looked around for a landmark to place his whereabouts. "I'm out front of a place called 'Perfect Pour.'"

The signage was flashing in pink neon overtop the front door.

"I thought you were going home."

"I was."

"Are you okay, Mr. Samuels? Are you in trouble?"

"I don't know. Maybe. Probably."

"Mr. Samuels, listen to me. You need to get off the streets. Go inside the bar and wait. I'll be there in a few minutes. Don't go anywhere."

"Thank you, Ilsa K."

Her face disappeared from the videophone. He

~ ☾ ~

hung up and stared at the entrance to the bar.

The interior of the club was dimly lit and hard to navigate through the tint of his sunglasses, but he didn't dare take them off. He walked carefully towards a corner booth near the back and slid into the soft cushion bench. He felt protected in the booth, out of view from the cluster of tables that were arranged in a neat grid pattern on the opposite side of the bar. It appeared great pains had been taken to set up the tables in perfect symmetry – each table in its spot, accompanied by four well-placed chairs, all neatly tucked.

Beyond the organized cluster was a section of single seats with ideal sightlines to a dark stage, which was presently closed off by a curtain. Left of the stage, a finely groomed bartender took inventory of liquor bottles organized by brand behind the horseshoe-shaped countertop. The man moved in time to quiet jazz music piping in from the overhead speakers, ensuring every bottle was positioned with the label outwards, and that all the bottles were clean and tightly packed side-by-side.

A swath of bright light cut through the darkness as a group of men entered from the street, laughing jovially as they filled the seats nearest the stage. The men, with their brown hair and dark-colored business suits, all looked strikingly similar. They were like clones of one another. Stanford watched them for a moment and wondered if they had enjoyed their time at the hanging. They laughed and slapped each other on the back like they had just been to an exciting sporting event.

An approaching woman diverted Stanford's attention. Her brown hair was cut into a bob and she wore a white T-shirt displaying a picture of a frosty mug of beer on the front, with an apron tied around her waist.

~ ☾ ~

"I didn't see you come in," she said. "You're hidden back here."

"I just arrived."

Stanford's stomach swirled, and he felt the beginnings of a cold sweat breaking out on his forehead.

"What can I get you?" she asked.

"I'm waiting for a friend."

"If you want to wait in here you have to order a drink. It's our policy. Colonial Lager is on special."

"That will be fine."

When she turned to fetch his drink he saw the back of her T-shirt: *We pour a perfect pint.*

He leaned against the headrest and tried to relax, but the pain in his stomach wouldn't allow it. Relief came only when he sat with a straight back, taking the pressure off his abdomen. Picking up the cocktail napkin to dab his sweaty forehead, he noticed the surface of the table was composed of a smooth reddish wood that seemed foreign in both texture and color; when he bent over to take in the scent, he was reminded of the giant trees surrounding the collie farm where he had travelled with his mother all those years ago.

A pang of sadness struck him as he thought about the old boy in the house all alone. Would the robot take care of him? He tried to picture his mother's face but it was blurred by time.

He sat upright, shaking the images from his mind, and looked around at the Perfect clientele. He suddenly realized that, with the exception of the Eradicators, he was one of the only colonists who could describe the subtle differences between a mutant bar and a Perfect bar. In a mutant bar, the like mutants sat together and dressed according to their own personal tastes, or to mask a certain mutation. By contrast, all the men in the Perfect bar were dressed the same and appeared physically similar. They dressed in business suits with

~ ☾ ~

crisp white shirt cuffs and collars neatly tucked in place; silver cufflinks with smooth black decals adorned the fabric. Perfectly polished black shoes pulled the look together. Their dark attire matched the darkness of their hair and eyes.

The raucous behavior, however, was comparable on both sides of the walls. The raging male hormones were especially evident when the curtain raised at the front, and a woman wearing only g-string underwear and a bra made of bird feathers came prancing out with a big smile on her bright pink lips.

She worked the men into a virtual frenzy, strutting around the edge of the stage in high heels. Twisting her long blond hair with her finger, she teased the Perfects in the close seats, surprising them by running to the opposite side of the stage and swinging around a pole several times until she came to rest on the floor with her legs split in opposite directions.

The men clapped and hooted but the performance was not over. She got to her feet and took hold of the pole once again, this time turning herself upside down and holding her body motionless for several moments, exhibiting an astounding degree of muscle control, until finally sliding back down to the floor and allowing the men to shower her with applause.

She stood up and took a bow. Her nipple tassels spun around like tops attached to her breasts.

The Perfects went wild.

One man near the stage was particularly rowdy. He waved his mug at the android stripper in an attempt to get her attention, slopping beer onto the stage. Noticing his miscue, he stumbled drunkenly towards the bar to get a refill, glancing in the direction of Stanford's table on the way. Stanford tried to avoid eye contact, but the man staggered over. When he arrived he leaned on the table for support and stared directly into Stanford's sunglasses.

~ ☾ ~

"Are you enjoying the show?" he asked through slurred speech.

Stanford nodded. "Yes."

"I bet you'd enjoy it more if you took off those glasses."

Stanford glanced around the bar, hoping the man would take the cue to leave. But the man was too drunk or too ignorant to take social cues.

"Why do you wear sunglasses in the dark, anyway? It seems kind of strange."

There was a strong odor of liquor emanating from the man.

"The strobe lights bother my eyes," said Stanford.

"That android has a beautiful figure. You should see her without your glasses."

"Maybe I will for the next dance."

"You'd like to make love to her, wouldn't you?"

"I never thought of it."

The man emitted an intoxicated belly laugh. He nearly lost his balance but held onto the table top until he regained his footing. "All Perfects think about it. It's the best part about being a Perfect. We don't have those sex laws like the mutants. I'd hate to be a mutant, wouldn't you? Always told who you can and can't have sex with. It would be a bloody bother, as far as I'm concerned. I just want to do it when I want to do it, know what I mean?"

Stanford nodded.

The man stared towards him with droopy drunk eyes.

"What's your name, friend? I haven't seen you before."

"Stanford."

"Let me buy you a drink, Stanford."

"I appreciate it, thank you, but I'm waiting for my ride."

"Leaving so soon? What better place is there to be than here?"

~ ☾ ~

Out of the corner of his eye Stanford saw a puddle of light flood in through the front door. Ilsa K stood in the midst of it.

She spotted him instantly and waved him over.

Stanford nodded towards the drunk Perfect. "I have to go," he said. "It was a pleasure meeting you."

"Oh, I get it. I don't blame you for leaving with a broad. She's a real nice catch, Stanford!"

Ilsa K didn't say a word until they reached her cherry red sedan hovering over the sidewalk directly outside the bar.

"I'm parked illegally, Mr. Samuels."

As he got into the car he looked over at Ilsa K and noticed she was not smiling.

"Thank you for coming," he said.

"If I were in your position, I wouldn't fraternize with the locals, Mr. Samuels."

"I wasn't fraternizing. I was under attack by a perfectly drunk man. Perfects clearly don't metabolize alcohol any better than mutants."

Ilsa K put the car into gear and pulled away from the curb. "Buckle up, please."

She was silent the rest of the way, staring straight ahead the whole time.

Stanford talked to himself to break the tension. "I'm a fugitive in a bright cherry red sedan that was illegally parked outside a strip bar. They'll never find me."

~ ☾ ~

8.75

Ilsa K's apartment was a thirty-minute drive from the downtown core, but neither Ilsa K nor Stanford uttered a word for the entire trip. When notice of the Tech Terrorist's execution came on the radio, Ilsa K reached forward to turn it off.

Ilsa K was not the same woman he had met earlier. She seemed frigid and lifeless. He was relieved when she brought the sedan down into the parking lot of a tall residential building. Maybe the change of scenery would return the woman he had known.

Stanford struggled to keep up as she led him through the narrow hallway to her suite. This was not the hallway with plush carpet and beautiful décor of the Personal Associations building. The carpet here was trodden and old; the lighting was dim and uninviting. When they got inside she flipped on the overhead EM tubes and he noticed how starkly white her face was in contrast to her raven black hair. He had been drawn to her beauty since the moment he laid eyes on her, but it wasn't until he saw her this way – her hair down, haggard and unpolished, lip stick faded – that he felt the urge to kiss her. He felt instantly guilty.

"Is there something you need to tell me, Mr. Samuels?"

He felt a painful clenching in his stomach. "I just need to sit down."

"The living room is through there."

The interior of Ilsa K's apartment was modest: a narrow galley kitchen, small three-piece bathroom, single bedroom. The living room was easily the largest

~ ☾ ~

room in the apartment, consisting of a couch, a small table with a few chairs for entertaining, and a video screen, which illuminated the darkness with an image of the Patron delivering an impassioned speech before masses of Perfects. The sound was muted, but the leader's intensity was evident in his deliberate movements and wide, piercing dark eyes.

All four walls adorned prints depicting wildlife in their natural habitats. One print in particular caught Stanford's attention; the frame was so large it nearly filled the entire south wall. It was a magnificent Great Horned Owl perched in a tree amidst a dense forest – the looming eyes like fluorescent yellow plates regarding him as he sat on the couch.

Ilsa K called from the bedroom: "Make yourself comfortable, Mr. Samuels, I'll be out in a minute."

The rumbling in his stomach seemed to reverberate into his chest cavity and squeeze his lungs, and for a brief moment he had difficulty breathing. He told himself to be calm and tried to breathe through his nostrils.

Ilsa K finally appeared, dressed casually with her hair like a black waterfall over her shoulders. When she sat down next to him he noticed the warmth had returned to her features. He couldn't help but envision Sarah in her place.

"You look beautiful," he said.

Ilsa K smiled. "Thank you." She brushed her hand along his sweaty forehead. "Tell me what's wrong with you, Mr. Samuels. Are you ill?"

"Call me Stanford."

"Okay, Stanford. Tell me what's wrong."

"I'm just tired, is all."

"What happened today? Why didn't you go home?"

Stanford let his eyes roam back to the video screen. He could feel the Patron's beady eyes burrowing into him, calling him out for the intruder he was.

~ ☾ ~

"Can you change the channel?"

"Do you want me to turn it off?"

"No, change it to something peaceful."

She leaned forward to switch the channel with the tiny control module on the coffee table. The video screen switched to images of the artificial environment – desert, grasslands, prairies, tropical rainforests; they were still photos that changed every few seconds. He felt a sense of relief.

"I defected from the mutant colony," he said after a time.

"Why, Stanford?"

"There's nothing for me there now. I thought maybe I could come here and spend my last few hours with you."

"What do you mean: last few hours?"

"I don't want to talk about all the things that have happened up till now. I just want to experience something nice."

"I don't understand. They'll find you, Stanford. If they find you, they'll kill you."

Stanford looked back into the haunting eyes of the owl. He felt himself sinking into the dark centers.

"We have to get you back. You can't just run away, Stanford. That's not a way to live."

Stanford looked back at Ilsa K and removed the business card from his breast pocket. He extended it towards her, bottom-side up to reveal the sketch of Saturn.

She took the card and looked away.

They sat in the dim living room like that, both staring at the various landscapes on the video screen in silence, and it was entirely pleasant to hear nothing but the slow rhythmic breathing of each other's bodies.

After a moment Ilsa K spoke. "Did you only call because you were intrigued?"

"I called because you were kind to me. It felt good to be near you. Did you not want me to call?"

~ ☾ ~

"Of course I did."

"Why?"

"I like you, Stanford. I liked you as soon as I met you. There's something about you that is very attractive to me."

"But why risk your safety?"

She hesitated. "I recognized your name on the guest list. I wasn't sure at first." She hesitated again.

"Go on, please."

"This might be hard for you to hear, Stanford. Sarah and I were friends before she was selected for coupling. We grew up together not far from here. We took classes at the Perfect University. I never envisioned a time we wouldn't be together. I was devastated when she left because I had never lived without my best friend, but at the same time I was happy for her to be chosen as an Eradicator, maybe even a bit jealous. We always had a friendly competition to see who would be the first to be coupled or the first to be granted adoption. They made it sound like eradication was guaranteed. It was such a privilege to be selected and I was happy for her, I really was. But it was hard to see her go."

A piercing pain shot through Stanford's stomach. He doubled over in agony.

Ilsa K rubbed her hand along the length of his spine. "Can I do something for you?" she asked.

"No. Go on, please."

"Are you sure?"

"Go on," he repeated.

"I lost contact with Sarah when she left for the mutant colony. I didn't hear from her for two years. I had no idea what had come of her. That's the worst part of coupling. Communication is cut off to maintain the integrity of the experiment. As time went on I learned to live without her. I thought about her, sure, she was my best friend, but I treated it almost like she had died. I know it sounds stupid, but even though I knew I'd see

~ ☾ ~

her one day again in Salus, a part of me wanted to have a wake, just to achieve some kind of closure so I could move on. Nobody thinks about those things when they are selected for coupling. Everybody just thinks about the good things, about what an honor it is to serve the Policy. They don't think about the people they are leaving behind."

A tear ran down Ilsa K's pale cheek. She took Stanford's hand for comfort.

He could feel her trembling.

"So you can imagine my surprise when I was walking in the central sector a few weeks ago and I saw a woman who looked exactly like Sarah. I didn't know what to think; was she one of those new androids who replicate the dead, or was it really her? I couldn't bear to think that she had died, so I decided to approach her. When she saw me she broke down and cried. At that moment I knew for sure it was Sarah. My friend had come back."

Stanford squeezed her hand.

"She was scared, Stanford. We went out for lunch to talk. She had so much to say, she seemed frantic. She told me she had been sent back to the Perfect colony because she was infertile. She had no idea that she had a problem. She said she had gone to the doctor to inquire about her mutant couplet's test results and she was apprehended at the office. She said the worst part was not being able to say goodbye to her mutant husband. She told me her husband's name: Stanford Samuels ... a man with the eyes of Saturn."

Stanford's whole body felt numb. "What happened to her?"

"I don't know. She didn't know whether she'd be sent back to the mutant colony to live as a solitary, or if she'd be sent to the outer boundaries. She knew she was infertile and would not be allowed to stay in the Perfect colony. I didn't know what to do for her, so I told her she could stay with me, at least until things got sorted

~ ☾ ~

out. But she couldn't go anywhere, she said. They were watching her."

Ilsa K began to weep.

"I dropped her off at her place that night. She had a room rented in the eastern quadrant – just a temporary suite. She gave me the spare key and told me if I could do one thing, it would be to check on her the next day, just to make sure she was okay. When I returned the next morning her suite was completely empty, like nobody had ever set foot in there. Everything had been stripped, the carpet, all the furniture, appliances, everything. I could even smell new paint. It's like she never existed. I have no idea how somebody could disappear so quickly without a trace. I'm sorry, Stanford. That's why I gave you my number. When you left the tower today I decided that if you called, I'd tell you everything because you deserved to know. If you didn't call, then you would never have to feel the pain of my disclosure. I can't decide if I'm glad you called or not."

A tear streaked down from behind Stanford's sunglasses.

"I'm so sorry," said Ilsa K.

He stared forward at the video screen and slowly removed his glasses. He felt hollow inside as he turned towards Ilsa K with his mutant eyes. She didn't flinch.

"Your eyes are on fire," she said. "Does it hurt?"

"Only when I look in the mirror."

"I need to take you somewhere, Mr. Samuels."

Stanford was silent. He wiped the tears from his cheeks.

"I need to take you on a tour of the seventeenth floor of the Central Tower. I promised myself that I'd tell you everything if you called, but I don't want to tell you this. I want to show you so you can see with your own eyes."

"What is it?" His voice was weak and broken.

~ ☾ ~

"I do tours for lots of different high ranking Perfects, from business people to government officials. Once in a while I take them to the seventeenth floor where the incubators are stored. There are hundreds of babies up there, maybe thousands, all waiting for adoption."

"Why are they taking them so young? They have to be five to be eligible for adoption."

"None of the babies are born of coupling, Stanford. They are all offspring of the new experimental androids. Do you realize what could happen to me were someone to find out what I'm telling you?"

Ilsa K shifted her body to the far side of the couch so she could see him entirely. "I'm telling you this because I feel sorry for you, Mr. Samuels, and you were coupled with my best friend."

"But what does all this have to do with the babies?"

"Oh God ... this is really hard."

She began to weep again.

"Were you coupled with an android after Sarah disappeared?" she asked.

"Yes. Her name was Glenda." His voice cracked. "She looked so much like her."

"Stanford, are you aware that you have a child on the seventeenth floor of the Central Tower?"

"How do you know it's mine?"

"It has your eyes."

Stanford put his glasses back on. "Did Sarah know?" He began to retch as he held back tears.

"No," said Ilsa K. "Sarah didn't know."

Ilsa K could see that he was hurting. She moved close to embrace him.

"I want a child, Stanford," she whispered.

He tried to move away but she held on tight.

After a moment he said, "Why not wait for adoption? You've seen thousands that will become available."

"I want a child of my own," said Ilsa K. "I've been on the list for years. I want to be a mother the way God

~ ☾ ~

intended. If I wait to adopt I'll be forced to share it with the biological parents inside Salus."

Stanford broke from her grasp and shifted away. His voice was suddenly firm. "What about the Policy?"

"Oh, Stanford, I want a chance to eradicate your mutant gene," she said. "Please do this and I'll take you to your son. I'll take you to the seventeenth floor."

They sat in silence for a long while, veiled in the darkness, under the watchful eye of the owl. After a time Stanford was able to compose himself enough to think clearly.

"I can't," he finally said. "I can't do it to Sarah."

Ilsa K looked at him with pleading eyes. "Please, Stanford. You have to accept that Sarah is gone."

"You don't know that."

"She was a mutant in the Perfect colony. There isn't much hope for her, Stanford. It pains me to say that, but it's true. Besides, you moved on from Sarah when you accepted Glenda. I want to serve the Policy as much as you do. Please give me the opportunity to do it my way."

She moved close.

"I see the way you look at me. I can't imagine it will be entirely painful for you to give me what I want."

Stanford stood from the couch. "I'm grateful for what you've done, but I must go. Thank you for your hospitality."

"Go where? Out there? To suffer the same fate as your wife?" Her voice was suddenly incredulous.

"I'm sorry, Ilsa K."

Stanford walked towards the hallway, pausing to look at the scenic images of the artificial environment on the video screen.

From behind, he heard Ilsa K. "Don't abandon your son, Stanford."

He felt a moment of dizziness and leaned against the wall for support.

~ ☾ ~

Ilsa K approached from behind, running her hand along his back.

He cringed.

"I will take you to your child," she said. "But you must give me the opportunity to be a mother."

Stanford locked eyes with Ilsa K and thought about his son in the incubator, all alone. He imagined the child's unanswered cries. After a moment, he followed Ilsa K down the hall to her bedroom. Now he thought about Sarah, just like he did every time he made love. He thought about how much he had missed touching real human flesh, running his hands along the contours of Sarah's knees, calves, thighs, breasts, just as he did now with Ilsa K. Her curves were just right and he tried to contain the fire in his loins a moment longer, to savor another blissful moment inside her warm body, but he was weak and could not hold out. A tidal wave washed over his entire body, but he felt no relief. He felt only sadness and embarrassment. He had betrayed his wife for the chance to see his child.

Please understand, Sarah.

He rested his head on Ilsa K's chest. There was something strange about the drumbeat of her heart. It had a slow, unusual tempo.

"Are you artificial?" he asked.

"You tell me, Stanford. Does it feel different when you make love to an android?"

He listened now to the thumping in her chest until he felt his eyelids get heavy and then there was only blackness.

~ ☾ ~

9.0

When Stanford opened his eyes he saw the miniature bust of the Patron on the bedside table; it was a replica of the bust from the hallway in the Personal Associations building. He realized Ilsa K's place in the bed had been vacated. The bed seemed instantly cold and uncomfortable. It pained him to turn his neck so he could scan the room.

When he managed to sit up, he saw Ilsa K at the foot of the bed, her naked back to him, slipping into the dark-colored business suit she wore during their first encounter earlier in the day. She turned to face him as she fastened the buttons of her blouse.

"You're awake."

"How long was I out?"

"Not long – an hour maybe."

"Are you going somewhere?"

"It's my turn to do something for you, remember?"

Stanford cringed as he tried to straighten his back.

"We don't have much time before daylight," she said. "I can get us in the night security door if we move fast."

"You don't have to do this."

"Yes, I do. Now stop talking and get dressed."

Ilsa K turned on her heel and swiftly exited the room.

Stanford felt a dull ache radiating through his body as he put his legs over the edge of the bed. Sitting fully upright, he saw the business card on the bedside table at the base of the Patron's bust. He became almost hypnotized by the sketch of Saturn before Ilsa K's voice startled him from the other room.

"Let's go!" she yelled.

~ ☾ ~

It suddenly occurred to him the heat radiating through his body was not a symptom of his illness, but a product of dread. Confirmation of the existence of his own child caused a swell of emotions to mix and jumble inside him. The delayed reaction confused him, and the reality of being a father and the possibility that Sarah was out there, still alive, probably fighting for her life, nearly crippled him.

He fought the urge to sob – there was no more time for tears. He needed to see his child.

Out of the corner of his eye he saw Ilsa K standing at the doorway. The look on her face indicated she knew exactly how he felt.

As he held her gaze, he saw a single tear streak down her face.

~ ☾ ~

9.5

Ilsa K's cherry red sedan moved like a nocturnal predator through the barren streets of the Perfect colony. The great buildings stood like sleeping giants on all sides, threatening to awaken at any moment and stomp out the tiny intruders. Other buildings were in partial ruin. The normally busy streets were eerily quiet.

"Nobody comes out at night now. The war may actually work to our advantage," said Ilsa K. Her voice had taken on a grim tone.

Stanford stared out at the massive outline of the Central Tower that came into view through the windshield. It was magnificent and untouched by the war, as if it were indestructible. He saw the street sign on the corner of the intersection. They had arrived at Idyllic Avenue.

"You're going to have to duck down a bit, Stanford. There will be security androids patrolling the perimeter."

Stanford felt a fluttering in his chest as he hunched in the bucket seat. Sure enough, when the sedan made its way past the face of the building, Stanford spotted the glowing night-vision goggles of security personnel behind the giant iron gates surrounding the compound. The image of silent, hidden androids caused a wave of nausea to flow over him.

"Don't worry, Stanford. I have clearance through the rear. Just stay close and don't say anything. When we get to the door, step back and don't move. It won't know you are there."

"What won't know?"

~ ☾ ~

"Just do as I say."

The sedan came to rest in a small parking area at the rear of the Central Tower. Before Stanford could gain his bearings, he was led up a steep staircase to a fortified door marked "Security Personnel Only."

Ilsa K pressed her finger into an identification sensor and a camera on a serpentine neck protruded from the door and investigated her body from head to toe. Stanford stared at her face, sensing the panic she suppressed beneath the calm exterior. She had so much to lose, he thought, and she put it all on the line for a chance at motherhood ... a chance that had gone unfulfilled despite her allegiance to the Policy.

She looked straight at him now, her eyes trembling, and mouthed the words: "Don't move."

The serpentine camera moved back up her leg, along the contour of her thigh, waist, chest, neck, and finally, after taking an extra moment to investigate the features of her face, retracted into the cavern atop the door.

It didn't sense Stanford at all.

In an instant, the door opened.

Ilsa K stepped inside.

Stanford tried to keep up as she passed quickly through the dark lobby and made her way towards the elevator in the hallway. The only light came from a scant few security bulbs in the ceiling. Ilsa K found her way and pressed the button for the seventeenth floor. The doors opened almost immediately and they stepped inside.

Ilsa K gestured for him to hold onto the handrails as the elevator made its swift ascent to the seventeenth floor.

Stanford felt his stomach drop.

When they emerged from the elevator, she led him into a massive room housing row upon row of silent incubators.

"Be careful," she whispered. "Perfect children sleep

~ ☾ ~

through the night. We only have a few minutes until the nurses do their rounds, but if we wake a child, security will be alerted and a helix dog will be on us immediately."

Stanford stood motionless for a moment, overwhelmed by the number of incubators, not knowing where to start.

"They move the babies around on a regular basis," said Ilsa K, "so we have to split up and search. Look for identification number 40065. Move fast."

He watched Ilsa K move towards the far aisle and decided to start with the aisle against the opposite wall. He moved briskly, peering in at each silent baby through the glass lids. All of the babies were newborns, all identical. Was his child here? There were literally thousands of capsules with faceplates displaying random digital numbers. The room was so large to accommodate the incubators that he could not see one side from the other. He felt a sense of hopelessness wash over him.

As he frantically peered inside each capsule, he heard Ilsa K's voice from somewhere behind: "Stanford, come here."

When he arrived he watched Ilsa K tap on the glass of an incubator marked with number 40065 in an attempt to wake a peaceful child from its slumber.

"What are you doing?"

She extended her hand to shush him. She leaned close to the glass case.

"Everything will be alright, dear child. You are so special and deserve the best life Salus has to offer. You come from a place of love, your mother and father could not have asked for a more precious gift. Your father is here now; open your eyes to him. Show him the beauty you possess. I wish I could sing you a lullaby that I learned from my mother. It's the least I could do, sweet child."

~ ☾ ~

Stanford stared intently at the baby. It was identical to every baby he had seen in the other capsules. He watched nervously as Ilsa K continued to tap on the glass until finally the baby stirred and opened his eyes.

Stanford was looking directly into the rings of Saturn.

"We have to go now," said Ilsa K.

He refused to move. "I can't leave." He looked at the child and thought about how Sarah would fall in love with the boy's eyes. The child's eyes were just like his – like the rings of Saturn she loved so much. All she ever wanted was a child like the one behind the glass. He heard her voice: *"You have beautiful eyes, Stanford Samuels, beautiful and mysterious like the rings of Saturn."*

This was their son. The baby they were desperate for. Not because of the Policy, but because Sarah wanted, more than anything, to be a mother. He longed to hold the child, to smell the sweetness of new life, to hand him to Sarah in a blanket cocoon. He wanted to prove to his wife that it wasn't a dream; the child was real – she was a mother! She would be so proud; so ecstatic. It's all she ever wanted ... but it was Glenda's son.

"I can't leave," he repeated. "I can't leave my boy here."

"You have no choice. He's no longer your child, Stanford. He is of special interest to the genetics division. He belongs to the Patron. Let's go."

Stanford resisted Ilsa K's urging until a flashbulb waved through the darkness; a figure approached through the aisles towards them. The cries of multiple children came from the capsules, echoing through the seventeenth floor.

"We have to go," said Ilsa K, in full panic mode now.

As the figure got nearer, the powerful body of the helix-sniffing dog came into view, rippling haunches moving through the shadows just behind its master.

~ ☾ ~

The dog lurched against the chain, snarling, impatient to get at the prey.

Stanford felt like his heart was being ripped from his chest as he fled from the room with Ilsa K. His paternal instincts were strong. Even with the threat of the dog, he wanted to stay with his child, to protect him.

Descending down the Central Tower, Ilsa K pinned Stanford against the elevator wall and kissed him passionately.

When she pulled away she looked deeply into the swirling rings in his irises. "It will be alright for you, Stanford Samuels."

She kissed him again and slipped a security pass in his pocket. "You'll need this."

"Where are you going?"

When the doors opened she ran out in a hurry. He could hear the sound of barking pursuing her.

He looked both ways down the hall, but Ilsa K was nowhere to be found.

A startling alarm began to sound and the lights in the lobby were suddenly ablaze.

He ran. He ran as fast as he could through the big lobby. All he thought about as he scrambled down the front steps of the Central Tower was Ilsa K. As security androids assembled in the courtyard, he could still think of nothing else other than Ilsa K. He felt no fear, no sadness – no sense of anything. He could only think of the woman who had shown him so much kindness, the woman who had risked her life for him, the woman who had led him to his child.

When he reached the iron fence, he swiped the security pass to get through the hydraulic gate. Outside the compound, he continued running until his lungs forbid him to go further.

He collapsed on the front steps of an old church, struggling to catch his breath. A sharp pain stung his ribcage. His kidneys had begun to swell, causing pain in

~ ☾ ~

his lower back. The radiation was starting to eat him from the inside out.

He looked up at the church, praying for some kind of miracle from above to save him. What he saw was the face of the Patron, pieced together in the multicolored shards of the stained glass window. It was the face of a man ... not an all-powerful god like he was perceived by the colonists, but just a mortal man.

He began to laugh. It hurt to laugh.

He leaned back on the steps and stared up at the expanse of the deep black sky, wishing for the first time in his life for the companionship of a silent celestial body – a moon. He felt so utterly alone. He desperately wanted to hold his child.

Overhead, an owl streaked through the darkness, its giant wings spread wide open catching an air current that would take it to a better place.

And then it was gone.

~ ☾ ~

PART III: (PERMANENT MIDNIGHT)

10.0

Approaching the waterfall he could see the figure of the woman bathing in the shallow pool. Her long black hair hung in wet ropes all the way down to the rounded curve of her buttocks.

She turned as he neared the edge of the pool, brushing wet strands out of her pale face. She smiled when she saw him.

"Isn't it beautiful?" she asked.

"Yes. I love it here."

"You've been here before?"

"I was here with Sarah."

Ilsa K looked disappointed. "Oh," she said.

"Do you live as a solitary?" he asked her.

Stanford watched her step out of the pool, exposing her glorious body in full view.

"Yes," she said. "I've lived as a solitary my whole life. I don't mind it. This place makes everything feel okay."

She came close and ran her hand along his cheek. "But I like having you here with me. You have beautiful green eyes, Stanford. They are like the phosphorescence in the water."

She leaned in and kissed him. Pulling away she said, "We can help each other."

"How?"

"You can help me bear a child. I want to be a mother. Just like your wife, it's what I've always wanted. And I can replace the child you lost to adoption."

"Can we do that here? Won't we be caught?"

She took his hand. "Come with me, Stanford."

~ ☾ ~

She led him through the same tangled pathway into the underbrush where he had gone with Sarah. When they reached the clearing, she sat on the overturned log so he could view the entire splendor of her nudity. She seemed so natural there, like she belonged in the forest amongst the trees and the animals. She pointed towards the canopy at the small bird with black spots and an orange marking on its tiny, fragile head.

Stanford saw it too. "It's a Flicker," he said.

"Sometimes when I walk through here I close my eyes and listen to the birds sing," she said. "I want to bring my child here to listen to the music they make, just like when I came with my mother."

"You came here with your mother?"

"Yes. She taught me to appreciate the forest and all the creatures. I even appreciate the insects. They all contribute in one way or another. The ecosystem is a delicate balance. Without one thing, all things eventually die. My mother taught me that. It's because of her that I feel such a bond with this place."

"What happened to your mother?"

"Same thing that happened to everybody's parents back then. They were conscripted. They died in the war."

When he got on top of her he could feel her skin was cold and tense. She looked back at him with pupils that seemed inordinately small.

"Make love to me, Mr. Samuels."

Stanford pushed into her with ferocious intensity. She howled and tore at his back with her fingernails, gripping him tightly with her legs. He felt sick to his stomach as he entered her. He could feel her muscles relaxing underneath him, her flesh beading with sticky sweat that bonded them together. He closed his eyes and lay beside her on the forest floor in utter exhaustion.

When he opened his eyes Ilsa K was gone. He was no

~ ☾ ~

longer in the forest but curled up in the fetal position on the front steps of the church where he had collapsed. His forehead was stained with sweat. He turned over and vomited on the church steps. He knew the radiation had reached his mind and was causing vivid nightmares. The effect was worse than the sleep transmitter.

A scream of agony echoed through the night, startling him.

The scream came again. This time he traced the origin of the sound as coming from inside the church. His pain couldn't match the agony of the person who emitted the terrible cries from within, and he couldn't bear to listen to it any longer. He walked up the steps and pushed open the front doors.

Inside was pitch black, and for the first time in his life his eyes worked to his advantage, glowing brightly to create a lighted path through the pews. His eyes burned stronger than ever before.

The radiation has reached my eyes.

He moved cautiously towards the faint sound of whimpering near the front of the church. As he got closer the cries became more intense, and he instinctively dimmed his eyes by putting on his sunglasses.

Walking through darkness again, he came upon a woman supine on the floor beneath the altar, her face obscured by a tangle of hair that did little to hide her pained expression. Between her legs, he could see the crown of a tiny head push out towards freedom until it finally broke free from the birth canal, followed by the afterbirth of broken fuses and stripped wires.

Suddenly it was over, and the church itself seemed to breathe a sigh of relief. He watched her chest rise and fall, slowly returning to an even rhythm. She sat upright and scooped the child into her arms. She was completely oblivious to Stanford's presence.

~ ☾ ~

Stanford was happy to keep the experience between mother and child. The scene made him wonder what it would have been like to lift his own child from the incubator – to hold him close and breathe the scent of newborn skin. What he would have given to see Sarah cradle their child in her arms, to see her smile like the proud mother she deserved to be. He yearned to see her asleep with the child pressed closely against her breast, its tiny lungs breathing in time to the heartbeat in her chest.

Watching the android with its new baby boy, he felt like an intruder. This was not his experience. His chance had passed and now he wanted to leave at once, yet something held him in place. Call it curiosity or envy or even anger. Yes, there was bitter resentment in him too. He felt all of these things as he took in the scene. This female android was as happy as any human mother could be.

He couldn't help but think how perfectly natural it all seemed, this human child spawned by an artificial mother. Was the child not human as he had first suspected? From behind the tint of his glasses, there was nothing he could see to suggest the child was abnormal. It even cried the way a genuine baby does after leaving the comfort and warmth of the womb for the first time. It was a human child, he could see, a perfectly formed baby boy who was expressing displeasure at being dropped into the dank, cold world of the dark church. One day the boy would call this woman "mother," and there would be nothing but natural love between them.

Stanford watched the child in the android's arms, and as the baby began to calm, he removed his sunglasses and pointed the glowing rays of his eyes towards the altar.

The mother looked straight into the spotlight.

"Are you a god?" she asked.

~ ☾ ~

Stanford stepped out from behind the pew. "I don't know what I am."

"Your eyes are unusual."

"I don't know what's happening to me."

"They are like beacons in the night."

Stanford glanced at the child's precious face. "Is your baby human?"

The android nodded. "My baby is a miracle."

"What will you name him?"

She kissed the baby on the cheek with a tender love that could only come from a mother. In the next second, a bullet passed through her skull and blew off the side of her metallic cranium.

The android slumped to the floor with the baby screaming on her breast.

Stanford dropped to the ground and shuffled for cover behind the nearest pew. He saw a man in old military fatigues step into the beams of light cast by his mutant eyes. The man, wearing a bandana over his face, ignored Stanford and walked directly to the android. He nudged the lifeless torso with his boot before slinging the assault rifle over his shoulder and leaning over to pick up the child.

When he stood back upright he looked directly into the origin of the spotlight.

"What are you doing here, mutant?"

Stanford was unable to speak.

"You're a long way from the colony, mutant. You can't stay here. The Militia is patrolling the area."

The soldier turned around and walked out of the church with the screaming child pressed to his chest.

Stanford waited until the man was gone before coming around from behind the pew. He looked at the devastated face of the android on the church floor. Black fluid leaked from the gaping wound, forming a puddle around the metallic head. He could see the tiny dots of her pupils slowly constrict until they

~ ☾ ~

disappeared completely, leaving two white dead eyes. He knelt down beside her and closed her eyelids with his fingertips.

"I'm sorry," he said. "You didn't deserve this."

He felt numb as he stepped over the dead robot on his way out of the church.

~ ☾ ~

10.5

A caravan waited on the street outside the church. Faces covered with bandanas peered out the side windows to get a look at the man with glowing eyes.

The assassin stood at the bottom of the church steps, the baby inconsolable in his arms.

"Come with us, mutant."

"What if I want to stay?"

"It would be a disservice to the cause if we left you here. We've dedicated ourselves to saving mutants, not leaving them to the helix dogs."

"Who are you?"

"We're the Tech Terrorists, who else?"

"Where are you taking the child?"

The assassin made his way back up the staircase towards him.

"Get in the van," said the assassin.

Stanford noticed the assassin fingering a pistol in his hip holster. "I suppose I don't have a choice."

"I can tell you want to commit suicide, mutant. If I hadn't seen you inside, I would have gladly left you alone to do that. But with eyes like that, you are hard to miss. You're our responsibility now. What you do after we take you out of here is up to you, but we're extracting you whether you like it or not. I suggest you make it easy on yourself."

Stanford pointed his shining eyes directly on the screaming child.

"What's your name, mutant?" asked the assassin. "And how did you get those glowing eyes?"

"I'm Stanford Samuels. My curse ... is evolving."

~ ☾ ~

"Well, Stanford Samuels, you can stand there and let those eyes shine like an SOS for the Militia and get us all killed, or you can get in the van. I can assure you the rest of the terrorists inside that van will not react kindly to your poor choices."

"How will we get back through the wall?"

"We have our ways, Mr. Samuels. This isn't my first day on the job."

Stanford watched the man walk back down the steps and take the baby through the side door of the caravan.

He looked around at the streets from atop the church steps and could hear sirens nearby. An explosion rose up in the distance like a brilliant flower blooming in the night sky.

He walked down the steps, and when he reached the caravan he poked his head through the side door to get a look inside.

The passengers, all wearing scarves to conceal their identities, raised their hands in unison to block the glare of his glowing eyes.

"Can you turn those things off, Stanford Samuels?" asked the assassin.

Stanford removed his sunglasses from his breast pocket and put them on his face. Through the tinted lenses he could barely make out the figures that filled the seats. He climbed aboard and sat down across from the assassin.

The assassin addressed the crew.

"This is Stanford Samuels. He's hitching a ride back to the mutant colony. He's not unlike us, for he too has a curse. I don't think I have to tell you what it is. Let's all make him feel comfortable."

Stanford could feel the caravan rise off the ground and begin moving through the dark quadrant. As the vehicle hummed along Stanford watched the assassin place the screaming child in the arms of a female crewmember. Within moments the caravan was peaceful.

~ ☾ ~

"She's our resident mother," said the assassin. "She has a special touch."

The assassin reached up to remove his bandana; now Stanford could see the red, swollen blisters that covered every inch of the man's face.

"Not a pretty sight, is it? I bet you don't feel so badly about your curse now, do you? Can you feel your pity evaporating? Have you ever seen a physical up close?"

"No." He tensed as he recalled the scene at the hanging square.

"Well, get a good look. Every one of us was touched by nuclear radiation in some form or another. They bombed our camps and banished us to the outer boundaries because they couldn't stand the sight of us. Not only terrorists, but innocent civilians who were accidentally nuked were cast out of the civilized colony. They didn't want the constant reminder of what they had done. Our children suffer to this day, born with birth defects that would make your stomach churn. You've never experienced horror until you've seen the scars behind these bandanas. Forgive us for not serving the Policy."

The assassin looked around at the rest of the terrorists. "Reveal yourselves," he commanded.

Each mutation seemed worse than the other. Missing noses, missing ears, gaping sores, open blisters, unimaginable horrors. These were the people he had heard about, sent to live in radioactive camps in the boundaries beyond the civilized colonies after the first war, left to die amongst the ash dunes. These were the men and women who deserved his pity, but he couldn't help that he had none to give. They were ghosts to him. The only discernible emotion inside him at this moment was disgust. Maybe he was a bad man, maybe he deserved to suffer as they had suffered. The only pity he felt was for the dead mother in the church, and for the baby who would grow up believing that the severely

~ ☾ ~

burned face of the resident mother belonged to the woman who birthed him.

The pain he felt in his stomach grew more intense by the minute. It was only a matter of time before he would go into toxic shock, but suddenly the idea of leaving the ugly world behind seemed like the best idea.

Every time I find a symbol of beauty – whether Ilsa K or my child in the incubator – I am bowled over by something sick and ugly. Why are the ugly images so much more prominent in my mind? Why can't beauty be the dominant one?

Unable to look at the faces of the physicals, he stared out the dark window to watch the contaminated desert. The sands were dark and quiet and they put him at peace. If he made it back through the walls alive, he could die in his own home with the old boy at his side. Was that a tear rolling down his cheek? He pictured the old boy all alone. When he looked at the woman holding the child, he saw her eyes were moist and he knew that she had compassion for him. The resident mother, whose face had been severely scarred by radiation during the first nuclear war, had sympathy in her heart for him. She, who had suffered unimaginable pain and loss, shed a tear for a man who looked back at her with only fear and repulsion.

The voice of the assassin broke the silence.

"Her name is Janice, in case you're wondering. That baby in her arms is as close to real motherhood as she will get. The radiation left many of our people sterile. We built our numbers back up slowly, but we are not what we were. What we lack in size we make up for in resolve. Call us rogues, call us thieves, call us terrorists; you can even call us murderers. This is our reality. Her name is Janice."

The assassin gestured towards the front of the caravan. "The driver's name is Alex. His co-pilot is Peter, but we call him Little Pete. And that's Michael

~ ☾ ~

and Jack and Junior and Joshua over there. The man next to you is Reid, and next to him is Max."

Stanford glanced at all the physicals as they were introduced.

"I see how you look at us, Stanford. But remember we were normal once – normal people with normal lives without the ugly scars. We lived among you. And you didn't look twice. We all have names. I won't ask you to repeat them back."

Stanford stared at the blistered face of the assassin. "You speak to me as if you are above reproach, but then tell me why you killed the android."

"That woman was a fourth generation birth-bot, designed to pop out as many little genetically perfect babies as her artificial ovaries can handle. Her, and those like her, are the latest invention churned out by the Personal Associations Division, created with one purpose: to populate the Perfect colony with eradicated children every time they conceive. They are better than the previous models because they are the first to yield near flawless results. They are correcting the chromosomes, Stanford, and they will fill Salus with a whole new generation of Perfect people. The population problem is well on its way to being solved, and soon the androids will be pulled from the mutant colony and reprogrammed to copulate exclusively with Perfects. The Patron will have no use for mutants any longer. As long as those androids continue to make perfect little babies, there will be no room for mutants under the dome."

"You don't know that."

"Get your head out of the sand, Stanford. They don't need us anymore. You saw the android with your own eyes. The child is human! Look at it! A healthy human baby came out of that synthetic robot designed to look like a woman. Don't doubt your eyes, Stanford. You can choose to ignore it or you can help us take our place

~ ☾ ~

back. If the mutants want to get to Salus, we need to eliminate those fertile androids."

"What is it to you? Physicals won't be granted entrance to Salus."

"Don't underestimate us, Stanford."

"What will you do with the child?"

"We'll take the child to the tent city in the outer boundaries. Janice will care for him as if he was her own. The child is a part of our family now. We will give him the love he deserves. We are capable of that, despite what you may think."

Stanford looked through the windshield as the caravan skirted across the desert. Up ahead he could see what appeared to be a hole opening up in the desert floor, the sand pushed aside by a trap door in the ground. He felt the caravan slow ever slightly as it approached the hole before being swallowed up by the gaping mouth in the ground.

It was as if the bottom had dropped out as the passengers plummeted into the bowels of Ultim. Stanford held tightly to the armrest, his vision completely obliterated by the darkness. Soon the caravan achieved a controlled speed and advanced evenly through blackness, as if along a track.

Now, suddenly, lights illuminated the tunnel. Glowing red bulbs attached to scaffolding against the inner walls of the underground portal lighted the way. Through the side windows Stanford could see men – mutant workers with protective goggles and heavily insulated coats – using heavy machinery to drill a network of tunnels further into the Perfect colony. The giant machines looked like oversized corkscrews churning into the rock walls. Sound barriers had been erected over the active sites, nearly eliminating the sounds of burrowing.

There were multiple arteries attached to the main tunnel, shooting off in all directions, all lighted by the

~ ☾ ~

strings of red bulbs. Stanford watched the physicals work like a hive of bees, boring into the sides of Ultim with the massive corkscrews. They appeared like subterranean cave creatures, their skin glistening with the sweat of hard labor. The scene was unlike anything he had ever seen, yet the red lighting and the deformed features of the physicals reminded him of one thing. He turned to the assassin. "Is this Hell?" he asked.

The assassin glanced back. "Hell is up there, Mr. Samuels ... on the surface. These tunnels are the way out."

"Is there a way out of Hell?"

"We've spent the better part of thirty years creating this underground network between the two colonies. It's our secret refuge from the Militia and our safe passage through the walls. These caverns extend from the mutant colony all the way to the downtown core of the Perfect colony. They give us a distinct advantage when we wage our attacks."

"So there will be more death."

"There always is," said the assassin. "We need to secure our place in Salus by force."

"You claim that you fight for mutants. Then why have you been attacking the mutant colony?"

"It's a matter of putting the enemy on edge. There is strength in unpredictability. We rely on our Intel to tell us where the mutants are and where the androids are. If they happen to be in the same place, we must make a choice. Sometimes that choice is to sacrifice the mutants to further our cause. There are casualties in every war, Stanford. It's the only way to achieve our goal."

"I was right then." Stanford looked out the side window again.

"About what?"

"This is Hell."

The assassin was silent.

~ ☾ ~

Stanford glanced at the child in the resident mother's arms. The child was fast asleep, even as the caravan increased speed and began its ascent towards the surface. In a matter of moments the vehicle passed through an opening in a grassy field on the outskirts of the mutant colony. As soon as they were through, the opening closed without a trace of what lay beneath.

"Welcome home," said the assassin.

The child in the resident mother's arms opened his eyes for a moment and then fell quickly back into a soundless slumber.

The caravan whisked through the downtown core and finally descended on the street out front of Stanford's house.

"This won't be the last time you see us, Stanford Samuels," said the assassin. "If you decide to take up the cause, we'd be happy to have you."

"I'll keep that in mind."

Stanford stepped away from the caravan as it lifted off the ground and slipped silently into the darkness.

Alone now, he turned to look at the silent façade of his house. It was so quiet under the fall of darkness that it roused a feeling of sadness within him. This was it, he thought. He would spend the rest of his life in the mutant colony. He would die here. There was no way to Salus.

Inside the foyer, the dog reared up in excitement and tried to lick his face. The robot aide appeared from the kitchen.

"We were worried about you, Mr. Samuels. Did the meeting go long?"

"Very long," said Stanford.

"Did everything meet your expectations?"

"We'll talk about it later."

"Okay, Mr. Samuels. You are tired after a long day. Are you hungry?" asked the robot aide. "I've kept your dinner warm on the thermal platter."

~ ☾ ~

"I'm famished."

As they made their way towards the kitchen the aide said, "Did you find an opportunity to say hello to the director for me?"

Stanford patted the aide on the shoulder like an old friend. "Let's talk about it later, okay?"

"I understand, Mr. Samuels."

They entered the kitchen through the archway where the meal waited on the table.

Stanford sat down. "What is this?" he asked.

"It's a roasted Flicker," said the aide, looking very proud, "with seasonal vegetables from the artificial environment. I picked it up at a vendor downtown while you were away."

"It's a bird?"

"Yes. They say the meat is quite succulent, a lot like chicken."

The dog roamed in and curled at Stanford's feet.

Stanford cut into the bird with his knife and took a bite. "They're right," he said. "It's very succulent."

After dinner he set the sleep arc on medium and crawled under the sheets. "I could sleep for a year," he said.

"Goodnight, Mr. Samuels."

The aide turned off the EM tubes; the arc shined brightly over the bed.

"Goodnight, old friend."

The aide stopped in the doorway and turned back. "I'm glad you decided to set the arc to medium. I don't like seeing you suffer in the morning."

"I no longer need the arc to induce my suffering."

"I'm sorry, sir?"

"Never mind, old pal. Goodnight."

Stanford felt the collie jump up on the end of the bed and curl up. He tried to remember the last time the old boy had slept on his bed. It was before he was coupled with Sarah.

~ ☾ ~

The last thing he saw in his mind's eye was the image of the mother android's tiny pupils staring at him from the church floor before they faded to white.

In his fatigued mind, the face of the android was superimposed with the face of Sarah.

~ ☾ ~

10.8

Stanford's eyes popped open as soon as the sleep arc went dim to indicate the end of the cycle. He felt remarkably refreshed considering the cycle had ended in the middle of the night, though the pain in his entrails remained overtly present. He clutched his stomach and looked towards the bedroom window. There was still darkness behind the curtains.

He smiled when he saw the old boy sleeping soundly at the foot of the bed.

Good old boy. You deserve some peace. Sleep for as long as you can. There's nothing to wake up for. Dream of the best of times.

"I trust you slept well."

The voice came from the aide, standing near the doorway.

"So far, yes, thank you," said Stanford.

The aide moved into the room. "Mr. Samuels, there is an urgent matter that we need to discuss."

Stanford threw back the sheets. "We can talk about it in the morning. I need to use the washroom. Why are you up so late?"

"It is morning, Mr. Samuels. You need to hear this broadcast. I recorded it from the radio a few minutes ago."

Stanford stopped in his tracks.

The voice of the Patron took over from the robot's mouth.

"Permanent midnight has arrived. This is something we anticipated since we landed on Ultim, and the moment of truth has come. I implore you not to panic.

~ ☾ ~

Even in the absence of sunlight, the temperature will hold for as long as it takes us to assemble in the terminals and board the fusion train for Salus. This is what we have planned for.

"As discussed many times over, the Perfects will assemble first and enter Salus in an orderly fashion. Each Perfect will be given a ticket to their new home in the wonderful new subdivision in the northern sector. The subdivision is complete with man-made lakes and green spaces for the whole family to enjoy. After each and every Perfect has been accounted for, we will begin the exodus from the mutant colony. This is the part that stings my heart, mutants, for only those who have successfully served the Policy will be granted entrance. There simply isn't room for everyone. As you well know, our new society under the dome will be free of the diseases and illnesses that have plagued mankind in the past. We cannot afford to permit incurable mutated chromosomes into the delicate ecosystem under the dome that could threaten the survival of our entire race. Our geneticists worked as hard as humanly possible to locate Eradicators for each and every one of you, but if you were not coupled it is because there was no possible way to eradicate. It is with a heavy heart that I say goodbye and God bless to those left behind. You will not be forgotten, mutants. You will live in the hearts of all of us forever. Thank you for attempting to serve the Policy and hold your heads high when you think of the contribution you have made to our new society. The new society will exist not in sickness, but in health."

Stanford pulled back the curtain covering the window and saw the darkness.

"I'm sorry, Mr. Samuels," said the robot aide.

Stanford sat down on the end of the bed next to the dog. He pushed his nose into the black and white fur of the old boy's neck and smelled the sweet scent that he

~ ☾ ~

was so familiar with. He ran his hand along the dog's head, pressing down the pointy ears, and saw the dog's eyes open to take him in.

"Come on, old boy," he said.

The dog licked his hand and eagerly followed Stanford down the hall to the foyer.

The aide took up the rear.

"What are you doing, Mr. Samuels?"

Stanford knelt down and gave the old boy one final stroke before opening the front door. "Go, old boy. Get out of here."

The old collie looked up at his master with plaintive eyes and whimpered.

"Get out of here!" yelled Stanford.

The dog wouldn't leave so he gave it a little kick to get him started.

With that the old dog walked reluctantly down the walkway, looking back several times until Stanford shut the door.

"Why did you do that, Mr. Samuels? The dog will die out there."

"No he won't. Animals are more suited to surviving in the wild than humans."

"It will freeze to death. The food supply will dry up."

Stanford walked towards the aide.

"What are you doing, Mr. Samuels? Have you gone mad?"

"I'm tired of your broca chip. It's for your own good, pal." Stanford depressed the power button on the back of the robot's cranium. "I'm sorry."

He patted the robot on the shoulder like an old friend.

Now, suddenly, Stanford was alone in the house for the first time in his life. He walked heavily back to the bedroom and curled up in the fetal position on top of the sheets. He felt sick inside as the radiation ate away at his organs. His stomach felt twisted in a knot; he

~ ☾ ~

clutched the flesh of his belly and squeezed it between his fingers as hard as he could, but the pain inside was infinitely worse. Yet nothing could compare to the pain of realizing that he was totally, utterly alone.

He closed his eyes. He was resigned to it now. He just wanted to go to sleep.

He began to sob uncontrollably. Then he screamed in agony.

Leave me be now, God. I came back because you willed it! Now leave me be!

~ ☾ ~

11.0

Stanford had no idea how long he had been sleeping.

He stood up from the bed and walked to the window to pull back the curtain. It was still dark outside. He wondered when the mutants who had successfully served the Policy would be summoned to the fusion train. It could be a day or more before the Perfects completed their exodus; then it would be the mutants' turn. He could already feel a chill in the air.

He entered the en suite and stripped out of his clothes. In the mirror he could see his eyes glowing like flashbulbs.

I must remember to tell the director that I can see in the dark.

He entered the condensation booth and sat on the meditation cushion. The mist surrounded his aching body but the pain that existed inside could not be soothed by the steam. He was bombarded by the nightmarish image of the dead android, its head blown apart on the church floor. The image made him feel worse than when he had entered the chamber. When the cycle ended he stepped out and vomited into the toilet. He looked around for the dog, half expecting the old boy to rush in and lick the moisture from the tops of his feet. He could feel his heart being squeezed in his chest.

He returned to the bedroom and sat on the end of the bed. He looked around, completely at a loss for what to do next. That's when he heard the sound of honking outside. He stood up from the bed and walked to the window. Pulling back the curtain he could see the

~ ☾ ~

headlights of the caravan as it pulled up to the curb out front.

He dressed quickly and exited the bedroom on the way to the foyer. The assassin smiled when Stanford opened the front door.

"You have been summoned," said the assassin.

Stanford immediately tried to close the door, but the assassin stopped it with his hand.

"There's nothing here for you now, Stanford. Look around. The suns have extinguished. What are you going to do now? There's nowhere to go."

"You're right. I'm staying here."

"Staying here for what? Staying here to die all alone? That's pathetic, Stanford."

"I've made my choice. I'm going to die in peace."

"I won't let you."

Stanford tried to close the door again but the assassin pushed his way into the foyer.

The assassin spoke firmly now. "We received Intel last night that a mutant has been infected with I-132. I've seen this before, Stanford. Infected mutant POW's were released to our camps in the outer boundaries during the first war. They were so radioactive their skin felt hot to the touch. Most died of heart failure within days."

The assassin looked directly at him.

"The radiation is making its way through your bloodstream to your heart. Do you know what it feels like to die from radiation poisoning? It attacks the cells of each organ, one at a time, until the system ceases to function. I've seen men die in battle in the most horrible, gruesome ways, Stanford. Limbs blown off. Wounds so large the organs literally fall out of the body onto the ground. The toughest, most macho soldiers have looked into my eyes and begged for their own death while screaming like schoolgirls. But I've never seen anything that comes close to suffering from I-132.

~ ☾ ~

What you're feeling now is nothing compared to what's coming. I pity you, Stanford. If you stay here you will regret it, I promise you. Let me help you."

"Why do you want to help me?"

"Because you are a mutant – and because you are a curiosity to our people."

Stanford stared at the man in silence.

The assassin spoke again. "My people think you are chosen."

"I've got nothing to offer you or your people."

"You offer what everybody wants," said the assassin. "You offer hope. If you're going to die, go out fighting. Join us and take your life back. The Policy made you this way, just like it made us the way we are. It stole our dreams, our freedom; now it threatens to choke out our lives. Let's do what we can to take it back. Let's take Salus."

Stanford's legs buckled.

Now, supine on the foyer floor, he stared up at the assassin through blurred vision. He turned his head to look at the photograph of his wife on the wall. If this was the last image before death, he wanted the vision to be of his wife Sarah.

She was beautiful. Her soft face stared out from the portrait, so innocent, enveloped by her long brown hair.

Oh how he loved her hair.

From her perfect chestnuts he could see a single tear brim over her lower eyelid and streak down the flesh of her cheek, dropping from the photograph onto his lips. He tasted the salty tear with the tip of his tongue.

"They told me they made her an android," he said, "but it was not her."

He heard the voice of the assassin return: "We'll hunt down the android. We'll make it right."

"So many promises ..."

"Stay with me, Stanford."

Everything went as black as permanent midnight.

~ ☾ ~

11.3

The caravan moved silently through the vacant quadrant. Anarchy had been unleashed in the colony, and it was safer for the mutants to remain indoors until the Patron gave the signal to assemble at the terminal.

As for those who failed to serve the Policy, the countdown to the end had officially commenced. Would the solitaries spend their remaining time with loved ones or would they choose to die alone? Were they resigned to their fate or would they fight futilely for survival until the bitter end?

In his mind's eye, Stanford saw Ilsa K under the waterfall. She looked at him and smiled.

"You have so much good to offer the world, Stanford. Wake up now and make your mark. Wake up ... wake up..."

When he woke his face was plastered against the frigid side window of the caravan. He felt angry when he first opened his eyes, realizing he had not died. Why would his body not go away peacefully? He had every reason to pack it all in and go to sleep forever, yet here he was, his body prolonging the feeling of utter despair in the cold confines of the caravan. Would the physicals kill him if he refused to go along? What did it matter anyhow? Wouldn't it be better to be murdered swiftly than to allow the radiation to continue to eat at him? He knew, even in the best case scenario, he couldn't hold out much longer. He would welcome the end. He just wanted the pain to go away.

As he sat clutching his chest, he could hear the

~ ☾ ~

engine slow. When the caravan came to a halt he looked out the window and saw the buildings in the downtown core. He recognized these buildings, and suddenly he realized he was still inside the mutant colony. He looked towards the assassin for an explanation.

"We got intelligence that a pod of androids is holed up in the hardware store across the street," said the assassin. "This will be your first operation, Stanford. Take this."

The assassin held an assault rifle towards the back seat. Stanford refused to accept it.

"What's the use of killing them now?"

"The androids will be summoned to the dome and they will continue to procreate inside Salus. We need to eliminate them."

Stanford remained still.

"Have it your way," said the assassin. "You can carry the walkie-talkie."

"Give it to somebody else," said Stanford.

"You carry the gun or the transmitter. You decide. Everybody else has a job."

With that, the side door slid open, and the soldiers moved quickly across the street to the front door of the hardware store. Stanford's vision went in and out of focus as he approached the storefront. He saw a blurry image of the mutant, Joshua, rattling the front door before breaking the windowpane with the butt of his rifle.

Shards of glass crashed down on the sidewalk and the soldiers entered through the hole with lightning speed.

When Stanford's vision cleared, he peered through the hole in the storefront but could not make out what was happening inside. He could hear sounds of shuffling and movement, then silence followed by the sobs of a woman.

He took off his sunglasses and illuminated the

~ ☾ ~

interior of the hardware store. The mutant soldiers aimed their rifles at a couplet and their small child. The woman had an obvious cleft lip. She appeared frantic as she clutched her offspring.

The Eradicator male stepped towards the soldiers with his hands raised above his head. "Please, don't take our little girl. We want to stay here, to be together as a family in peace until the end. Please have mercy on our family."

Joshua looked towards the assassin. "They aren't androids, boss."

"I can see that," said the assassin.

With that the soldiers lowered their guns and filed back through the broken window towards the vehicle.

The assassin ripped the walkie-talkie from Stanford's hand and screamed into it about misinformation and not making the same mistake twice.

Stanford was barely hanging on as he stood in front of the broken window. Inside, the family embraced in the spotlight beamed from his mutant eyes. Both child and mother sobbed uncontrollably.

The Eradicator looked at Stanford intently, saying nothing.

Stanford back-pedaled from the storefront, glass crunching under his feet. No words could make things better.

He placed his sunglasses back on.

It was pitch black again in the hardware store.

Maybe it was better that way.

In the darkness, he could hear the little girl ask, "Are they gone?"

"The men are gone now," said the mother. "Everything will be okay."

~ ☾ ~

11.5 (OUTER BOUNDARIES)

The physicals exited the side door of the caravan and started off towards the encampment in the desert. Dozens of military caravans, all fortified with heavy artillery, were parked near the entrance to the tent city. The boundary was fenced off with electrified barbed wire.

Stanford stepped out of the caravan. As soon as his feet touched the ground he bent over and vomited into the sand. Standing upright he saw the blotchy face of the assassin.

"You need to see the shaman," said the assassin. "You'll be dead in less than twelve hours at this rate."

Stanford felt a wave of vertigo wash over him and he collapsed to one knee, his glasses dislodging from his face and hitting the sandy terrain. The assassin rushed to his side.

"Put your arm around me."

Stanford's vision was blurry. Even sounds seemed distorted.

He leaned against the assassin as they made their way slowly through the entrance to the tent city. His eyes shone a path on the sand brighter than he had ever seen, and before him he saw the physical mutants rush from their tents to greet him.

They dropped to their knees as he passed by, bowing their heads and placing their hands together in prayer like supplicants. They worshiped him.

Stanford heard the voice of the assassin.

"They say it was foretold that the Messiah would arrive when the suns went out. They look into your two

~ ☾ ~

spectacular eyes and they see the new dawning of the twin suns."

"They always shine brighter ... right before they die." Stanford's voice petered out.

The supplicants lost their shape in Stanford's eyes; they seemed to melt upon the sand like candle wax pooling in a shallow dish.

In his ear he could hear: "Stay with me, Stanford."

They were inside a tent that glowed from a fire burning in the center. The assassin lowered Stanford onto a cot.

The shaman, in a faded cloak, sat on the other side of the fire. He looked at the strange man who had been delivered to his tent.

"Is this the man with the fire in his eyes?"

"Yes," said the assassin. "The iodine capsule has been in his system for more than twenty-four hours. It seems to have exacerbated the mutation in his eyes. He's in toxic shock."

"It may already be too late," said the shaman.

The old shaman stood up from the sand and rounded the fire to get a closer look. He peeled back Stanford's eyelids. The copper fragments suddenly appeared dim and lifeless. The stunning beams had extinguished.

"This man is almost dead," said the shaman. "Is he worth saving?"

"I believe he is," said the assassin.

The shaman stood up and walked to the other side of the tent and opened a small chest. He brought out a feathery green fern frond and laid it on the sand near the fire; then he returned to the chest and brought out a wooden mortar and pestle. He hummed to himself as he sat cross-legged in the sand and ground the leaf in the mortar.

"Why is he worth saving?" asked the shaman as he worked away.

"He has a presence," said the assassin.

~ ☾ ~

"What kind of presence?"

"A special presence. Like nothing I've ever seen."

"Could he be the one?"

"I don't know. But I've seen how they worship him. They need hope. It's worth it."

The shaman grunted and continued to grind the frond in the mortar.

When the leaf was prepared, the shaman walked back around the fire and knelt next to Stanford.

"How's his heart?" asked the shaman.

The assassin checked for a pulse. "It's weak."

"Tilt his head back and open his mouth," instructed the shaman.

With Stanford's mouth agape, the shaman tilted the mortar to allow the liquid from the crushed fern to drizzle down his throat.

"Talk to him," said the shaman. "Keep him with us. If he leaves us now, there is no hope that he will find his way back."

The assassin looked down at Stanford's pale, sunken face. He appeared to be on the edge of death.

"Do you hear me, Stanford? Don't stray too far. Follow the sound of my voice."

Stanford could hear the voice but it seemed so far away. He watched the twin suns dip below the grassy hill in the distance, but he could not see the owner of the voice. He cupped his hands to his mouth and shouted with all the force he could muster, "I can hear you! Where are you?"

Silence now.

He looked in the other direction and saw the boundary of the forest in the distance. There were birds and deer and snakes and squirrels in the forest, and all types of fungi and flowers and insects and broad-leafed plants. He remembered how Sarah liked to walk in the forest with her mother, losing herself amongst the giant trunks, flipping through the pages of her bird book to

~ ☾ ~

identify the lovely colorful birds that nested in the canopy.

Do the trees hold up the sky?

He smiled as he turned to look in the opposite direction at the boundary of the wide roaming plains where the grain was harvested, and where the jackrabbits and buffalo and coyotes roamed. He realized how alive he felt, how healthy and strong he was when he looked straight ahead at the edge of the savannah. Maybe one day he'd take a safari, he thought. There was no better time than now.

He'd never seen a lion or an elephant or a zebra in person. The idea of seeing these majestic creatures for the first time in his life excited him and filled him with power. Why hadn't he come to the environment sooner? This was the beauty he had been craving. There was no ugly here – no rot or sickness or disease. Who needed a Cleansing Policy when an environment such as this existed naturally? No one could touch him now. He was invincible.

He looked back towards the big hill and saw the black and white collie cresting the top and running towards him. The dog ran like the wind, churning his legs faster than ever. He was even quicker than before the reversals, like a vigorous young puppy again, and as the old boy got close Stanford could see the big wet tongue dangling out of his mouth.

"Come, old boy!" he shouted. "Come on!"

As it neared, Stanford dropped to his knees, allowing the dog to crash over him like a tidal wave. Stanford squeezed the dog in his arms and scratched his sides and the top of his head.

"I missed you so much, old boy. Thank you for coming back. We'll never be apart again. I'm sorry for what I did. You've always been there for me. Now you can count on me, too."

Stanford threw himself back into the grass to get

~ ☾ ~

away from the enthusiastic tongue. The dog was upon him again, and Stanford buried his face into the old boy's sweet-smelling coat.

As they frolicked in the grass, the familiar voice came from somewhere beyond the big hill.

"Can you hear me?" said the voice.

Stanford looked into the old boy's big gentle eyes. "I don't hear a thing, do you, old boy?"

The dog barked excitedly.

"Want to go for a walk, old boy?" he said, getting to his feet. "Why walk when we can run?"

Stanford and the old boy ran towards the forest. It felt wonderful to be alive, and it felt especially wonderful to be reunited with his lifelong companion. There was no reason to return to his old life. He was happy now. He knew he could manipulate this world the way he wanted; he could have everything he had ever desired but was denied in the colony. What was the purpose of returning to the old way of suffering? He wasn't going to acknowledge the voice that pursued him because that voice wanted to bring him back.

He entered the tangled bank with the old boy at his side. Together they walked towards the sound of the waterfall. When they got close he could see the naked figure of his wife cleansing herself in the cascade. Watching for a moment, he admired the contours of her body and wished he could freeze the image and stare at her for eternity.

He suddenly realized it was in his power to stop time and capture the image like a photograph, but doing so seemed indecent.

She sensed his presence and turned to greet him.

"Hi, Stanford," she said. She glanced at the dog. "The old boy came back."

"Yes."

"I guess you always knew he would."

"He's always been with me."

~ ☾ ~

She smiled. "You have a beautiful heart, Stanford Samuels."

She waded towards him.

"And your green eyes are so lovely."

As she stepped out of the pool to reveal every inch of splendor, Stanford caught sight of something floating in the shallow water that made his heart skip a beat. Was it a doll? He advanced towards the pool to get a better look.

"Don't mind it, Stanford," said his wife, trying to recapture his attention. "It doesn't matter now. We can be together – just you, me, and the old boy, like old times. We're a family again. This is what you've always wanted."

Stanford felt a pain surging in his chest as he knelt down at the water's edge. He stretched out for the object floating in the water and finally managed to reach it. When he brought it in he saw the bloated face of a drowned baby staring back; its eyes revealed hints of copper specks in the irises.

He pulled the child out of the water and quickly brought it to the shore to revive it. His efforts were futile.

He looked up at his wife. He could feel his eyes getting hot.

"Stanford, why are you so upset?" she asked. "Look at your child's eyes. We failed the Policy. This child was never a part of our family. Let's go back to what we had."

Stanford kissed the child on the forehead. He could still smell the scent of sweet skin.

"Let's be together, Stanford," said his wife. "Isn't it wonderful that we have this second chance? I can't believe how fortunate we are to meet up in Salus, just like we always talked about. Oh, Stanford, I love you."

The woman rushed towards him but stopped in her tracks when she saw the big yellow gun pointed back at her.

~ ☽ ~

"Stanford, what are you doing?"

"You lied to me." His hand was trembling as he struggled to grip the gun.

"What are you talking about?"

Just as she said it, he saw her pupils constrict to the size of pinpricks.

"I'm sorry, Glenda," he said.

Before he could pull the trigger a stray bullet tore a hole through the robot skull, sending Glenda flying backwards into the shallow pool of water.

Stanford quickly scanned the surrounding trees and saw the assassin standing between two massive trunks, gun drawn.

Stanford raised his bizarre yellow weapon and shot back, hitting the trunk several inches above the assassin's head; then bolted through the trees. The dog ran right along with him. He ducked under low-hanging branches and scampered over fallen logs until he reached the boundary that separated the forest from the savannah. He paused to look back but saw no sign of the assassin.

"He's no match for us here," he said to the old boy. "Shall we go find an elephant?"

The old boy barked excitedly.

Stanford advanced slowly toward the edge of the savannah while he caught his breath.

The setting suns cast a glorious glow across the grassy plains that stretched for miles in all directions.

He felt soothed now; his heartbeat had achieved a nice rhythmic pace.

The savannah seemed like it had been designed just for him. He felt at home here, comfortable for the first time in memory.

A few miles ahead he saw an acacia tree that seemed like the perfect place to rest. He started to run, glancing back to make sure the collie was following. When he and his loyal companion arrived at the tree, he

~ ☾ ~

collapsed at the base of the trunk and laughed in a state of utter delirium.

"I am home!" he cried at the sky.

The dog nestled down beside him.

"I feel so good, old boy. For the first time I feel like I'm in charge of my life. Nobody will tell me what to do. Nobody will make decisions for me. I have total autonomy. I will decide who I marry, how many children I can have, whether or not I can live out the duration of my life. I won't stand for people labeling me a freak. I won't be considered insignificant and weak and sick and flawed. Nobody can tell me I'm worthless and irrelevant, and force me from my home. From now on I answer only to myself. If somebody threatens my free will they will face the ultimate punishment. I will shoot them in the face with my yellow gun. Violence will send a message that I will not be kicked around anymore. Violence will preserve my sanctity and my freedom. From this moment on, I vow to kill in order to preserve my right to be a free man."

Stanford waved the twisted yellow gun in the air and howled.

"This is power," he said to the old boy. "This is freedom. I'll fight to the death before any person, artificial or genuine, threatens to rule me again."

Out the corner of his eye Stanford saw the assassin approaching through the wild grass. He took aim and pressed the trigger but this time the gun failed him.

The assassin came into full view.

"You're coming back," said the assassin.

"Coming back where?"

"Back from the dead," said the assassin.

Stanford stared at the bizarre yellow weapon in his hand and pointed it at the assassin again. "You can't take me."

He pressed the trigger over and over but nothing came out. He shrieked in frustration.

~ ☾ ~

"Give it a break. Do you think I wanted to kill the android, Stanford? Do you think I get a kick out of what I do? It makes me sick. I hate myself. Look at me. My face is a mess. I'm disgusting to look at. Don't you think I know what you are thinking when you look at me through your eyes? I didn't ask for this. I am who I am – just like you are who you are. It's not our fault. There's no justice in this world, Stanford. It's kill or be killed. The androids are making the mutants irrelevant by birthing children to boost the population, so we kill the androids and make ourselves relevant again. They add, so we subtract to keep an even playing field. It's as simple as that. I don't like it, but that's the way it is. We can sit here in some fantastical construct of your mind, hiding from those who have beaten us down and stolen our free will, or we can get back to reality and go take our spot under the dome by force. What do you want to do, Stanford Samuels?"

Stanford stared at the blistered face of the assassin. He could see puss oozing out a newly punctured pustule on the man's chin. He felt more sad than disgusted. He wanted the assassin to find happiness in a fantastical construct of his own making.

"I choose to stay here with my dog," said Stanford. "I'm tired of it all. I'm happy right where I am."

The assassin was silent for a moment. Then he said: "I'm bringing you back, Stanford. You don't have a choice. The cause needs you. When they look at you, they see hope. We can't let that go. It's the only thing we have left. I don't know who you are or even if you are special, but I know a symbol of hope when I see it, and I'm not letting it out of my sight."

Stanford leveled the gun at the assassin's forehead. "You don't rule me."

The assassin stepped towards the growling dog.

"There's someone waiting to see you on the other side, Mr. Samuels. I was going to keep it a surprise, but

~ ☾ ~

you give me little choice. Why did you have to ruin it?"

Stanford held the gun steady. "I could blow the back of your skull off from this range, even with an unsteady hand."

The assassin exhaled deeply, growing weary of the conversation. "Sure you can, but even if you blew my brains out, I'd only die on this plain. I'd be dead inside your head and what would that solve? They'd just send another physical in after you. You might as well save everybody the trouble. Besides, you're out of bullets."

Stanford looked at the dog. "I can't bring the old boy, can I?"

The assassin shook his head. "No. Aren't you the least bit curious about who is waiting for you? She's standing right next to me."

"Who is it?"

"Why do you think Sarah wasn't at the waterfall today?"

Stanford felt a surge of emotion well up in his throat. "Is Sarah with you?" he asked.

The assassin extended his hand. "Let's get out of here."

Stanford's legs felt weak and he leaned on the acacia tree for support. Before he took the assassin's hand he looked down at the old collie. "I'll come back for you, old boy. Wait for me."

Then he dropped to one knee and rubbed his hands along the black and white fur one last time. He patted the old boy on the flanks and said, "Go on now. Go run free."

The old boy barked and ran out of sight into the savannah.

Stanford put the strange yellow gun back into his pants pocket and took hold of the assassin's outstretched hand.

"Let's go," he said. "I'm ready."

~ ☾ ~

12.0 (SALUS)

When Stanford's eyes snapped open, he saw the faces of the assassin and the shaman looking down from overhead.

He felt a sharp pain stabbing his neck.

"Welcome back," said the assassin. "We didn't think you'd make it."

"Where did I go?"

"Only you know that," said the shaman.

"You talked in your sleep more than any person I've ever known," chuckled the assassin.

The shaman addressed the assassin now. "He'll be okay. He'll have his strength up before morning."

Stanford watched the shaman walk slowly out of the tent. He focused his eyes on the assassin who sat down beside the smoldering fire.

Stanford's throat was dry; his voice was raspy and weak. "What happened?" he asked.

The assassin looked directly at him and saw Stanford's eyes were calm.

"The fern was used as a general anesthetic. They grow out here in the desert. We don't know exactly how they work, but they do. You were under for a long time."

"How long?"

"You were out for over three days, Stanford. We didn't think you'd come back. The shaman said you were gone longer than anyone he has ever tried to cure. You were fighting to remain in a coma. You didn't want to come out of it. You even started to negotiate. You said you'd only come back if you could see Sarah."

Stanford felt numb.

~ ☾ ~

"Is she here?"

The assassin shook his head. "You were out of it. The shaman used a lot of the hallucinogen to sedate you while we pulled the implant out of your neck. We needed to get you back by any means necessary. Do you realize how lucky you are to be alive?"

Stanford looked at the assassin for a long time. "You lied to me."

"We saved you."

Stanford tried to lurch towards the assassin, to get his hands around the man's neck, but his muscles were weak and he collapsed back onto the cot. "I would kill you if I could." He began to sob. "You call this being saved?"

"We had to tell you what you needed to hear," said the assassin, "or you'd die. Sarah is gone. But your child is out there, Stanford. A child who will be your successor and lead us long after you are gone. This is bigger than you or me. We needed to get you back. You're too important. Your child is too important."

Stanford stared at the peaked ceiling of the tent, feeling his chest rising and falling as he inhaled the smoke from the fire. Finally he looked at the assassin. "My child is out there ... in the darkness?"

The assassin nodded. "We need to find him."

Stanford wiped away his tears.

The assassin patted Stanford's thigh and moved towards the exit. "Something happened while you were out that may interest you," he said. "It's a significant victory for our cause. Would you like to see what we caught while we were out fishing?"

Stanford watched the assassin disappear though the flap in the tent. He remembered how painful it was to be alone but it was different now. He felt a bond with the assassin, and Stanford felt a renewed sense of purpose for the first time since Sarah had vanished. His child was out there in the dark and the cold. He had no

~ ☾ ~

way of knowing what role his child would play – if the boy was a leader or a god like these people seemed to think – but it didn't matter. He was a father now, and a father needed to protect his son. This was his mission. The yearning for death was gone.

The sharp stabbing pain returned in his neck as he turned to see two medics enter the tent.

"Would you come with us, please?" said one of the medics.

Stanford sat up carefully and allowed the medics to help him to his feet.

When he was outside the tent he saw a prisoner strapped to the grill of a military vehicle in chains. It was the director of the Personal Associations Division.

The assassin stood next to the vehicle. "A caravan picked him up outside the Central Tower. We were tipped off by a woman in the Perfect colony who said she knows you."

"What woman?" asked Stanford.

"She didn't tell us her name," said the assassin. "She called us from an anonymous audio transmitter. All she said was we should examine the man's chest."

The director struggled to get loose from the bonds, but it was impossible.

"Mr. Samuels," said the director, wheezing. "How strange it is to meet you all the way out here. I guess this means you'll be rejecting our offer of the Alice unit."

Stanford felt in his pants for the twisted yellow gun but it was not there. It had never been there.

"You've made a grave mistake, Mr. Samuels," said the director. "We were so close to eradicating your eyes. You could have been a standard of success. Instead you are less than nothing. You are some freak living with a bunch of other freaks in the desert, all on the verge of turning into popsicles. Congratulations. You're really moving up in the world."

~ ☾ ~

Stanford looked towards the assassin. "Let's see his chest."

The assassin gestured for the physicals to pull open the director's jacket.

Stanford had a view of a normal-looking torso, complete with chest hair, normal-looking musculature and ribcage.

"Your place in Salus could have been solidified, Mr. Samuels," continued the director. "Your propensity to multiply was strong. You procreated with Glenda almost immediately, and we have no doubt that you would have produced one, maybe two, eradicated offspring with Alice. You just needed to accept the offer and you'd be sitting pretty in your own personal paradise. Somewhere, somehow, you went wrong."

Stanford glared at the director. He could feel his eyes getting hot.

The director sneered. "I have a message for you, Mr. Samuels. It's from your ex-girlfriend, the brunette who worked for me. She was a real looker, but not a very good guide. She always seemed to go into rooms where she wasn't permitted. Her escapades finally caught up to her, I'm afraid. Do you really think it would be so easy to gain unauthorized access into the Personal Associations Division if we didn't allow it to happen? We wanted to see how far the both of you were willing to go."

Stanford moved within inches of the director.

The director chuckled. "It was hard to understand what she wanted me to tell you in between her pathetic sobs for mercy. I watched her through the bars of the dog kennel as she kicked and writhed to save her own life. She would have said just about anything at that moment, if only to live one more day. It was about the time when the helix dogs bit into her abdominal wall and pulled out her entrails that she gurgled something about her heart being genuine. I can attest to that. I held her heart in my hand before I let the dogs devour

~ ☾ ~

it. Can you imagine what it feels like to hold a fresh human heart in your hand? It was still warm, Stanford. The last beats were rippling out. I doubt very much she was the one who made that call, if that's what you're thinking. There wasn't much left of her pretty face when the dogs were done with her – poor girl."

The director spat in Stanford's face and cackled.

The assassin lurched towards the director but Stanford stayed him with his hand.

Stanford's eyes were ablaze like never before, casting the director in a brilliant spotlight.

"Your eyes are burning like hell fire, Stanford. You're a freak. You deserve to be out here in the cold with the rest of them. You're all freaks. You deserve everything that comes to you. I hope you all die slow, painful deaths. Serve the Policy! Serve the Policy!"

Stanford saw into the director's chest cavity like an X-ray. Inside were gearboxes and circuits surrounding a pair of normally developed human lungs.

He glanced into the director's eyes. "You're artificial. I can see inside you."

"Your eyes are cursed."

"Your lungs are real," said Stanford.

The director grinned. "There is so much you can't even begin to comprehend, Mr. Samuels. Androids are becoming more human every day. You should know that better than anyone. You could barely tell the artificial from your own wife."

The man coughed out a puff of black smoke.

Stanford flashed a look at the assassin.

The director continued to wheeze. "I'm living proof that artificial is always better, but we are so close."

"What did you do to my wife?"

"I'm done talking, Mr. Samuels. My shutdown feature has been remotely activated."

Trails of smoke seeped from between the director's teeth.

~ ☾ ~

"My allegiance is to the Patron. Hail the Patron! Hail the Patron!"

"He's programmed for non-disclosure, Stanford," said the assassin. "We won't get anything from him but lies to throw us off track. Let's deal with him before he shuts down completely."

Stanford was so close to the director he could smell his foul breath. He looked directly into the man's constricted pupils. "You asked me once what benefit my eyes brought me. You asked if I could see in the dark. I didn't realize until now that it's not the dark I can see through ... it's the bullshit."

"You're a monster, Stanford. You better hope you freeze to death before the Militia finds you. You'll be a frozen snack for the helix dogs just like your girlfriend."

Stanford turned to the assassin. "I've heard enough."

Just like that the assassin motioned for two of his assistants. "Take him to the tent and destroy him."

"You'll all die!" yelled the director through billows of smoke pumping from his interior. "You can't imagine the horrors that await you. You can't imagine what the Patron has in store for you. You are all mutants!"

The director fought bitterly against his executioners as he was released from his chains and dragged towards the tent.

"Hail the Patron! Hail the Patron!" he shouted.

Shrieks of agony exploded from inside the tent.

Then silence ...

~ ☾ ~

12.5 (CONCLUSION)

The physicals assembled at the entrance to the tent city, all masking their deformities with scarves, rifles slung over their shoulders.

The director's ravaged body was attached to the front of the caravan again, this time with his chest torn open to reveal the machinery inside. There was an empty cavity where the lungs had been. The man who had once been so powerful was reduced to a mess of broken wires and circuitry – an inert, obliterated machine.

The shaman stood on the roof of a military vehicle and shouted, "There is another god with shining eyes who has been taken from us without consent. This god is in the form of a child, ripped from our fingertips by the enemy under the cloak of night. Our mission is to find the god out in the darkness and bring him back. When we reach Salus, we must slay the androids that make us irrelevant. Find a way into the artificial environment, my children, for this is our only hope. Let this man lead you …"

Stanford approached the vehicle and turned to address the crowd. "My name is Stanford Samuels." He hesitated. "I'm a mutant, like you. My mutation gives me these glowing eyes. You people seem to think I have been chosen to lead you. I've never been a leader in my life. I didn't ask for this. I don't know how to lead men."

He hesitated again, searching for words. He spotted the resident mother watching on, holding the android's child affectionately against her chest.

~ ☾ ~

"I don't even know how I got here. But what I do know is that you saved my life. You gave me a second chance and I'm not going to waste it. I will repay you. I have a child out there. Maybe he's the leader you seek. I have no idea. All I know is that he's in the dark and he might be cold. I'm his father and I won't accept that. He had a beautiful mother and all she ever wanted was a baby to be proud of." His voice cracked. "She's not here now, but I'll be damned if I don't do everything in my power to get my boy back. If my mission helps you take your place in Salus ... then it's the least I can do. Let's go take back what's ours."

The physicals roared in approval.

"Piss on the Patron!" they shouted. "Piss on the Patron! Piss on the Patron!"

Stanford led the army of mutants on foot across the desert – his path through permanent midnight guided by the glare of his mutant eyes.

He paused briefly to look back at the assembled army, and saw the director's mutilated body plastered to the front of the caravan like a hunting trophy.

Where's your therapy room now?

They continued on foot across the landscape of sand dunes for several hours until they took up camp in the middle of the desert.

In the distance the sand finally stopped, replaced by a carpet of tall, vibrant green ferns that radiated a green mist high into the atmosphere – a glowing vortex in the pitch black desert.

Amidst the strange tangles of high plants, the uppermost crown of the Salus dome poked through the foliage, the majority of the structure hidden from view by the ferns encroaching on its walls. Having adapted to the infertile conditions, the ferns thrived and appeared as hungry beasts growing up the sides of the structure as if to devour it.

~ ☾ ~

Stanford stared at the dome with only one thought. He wanted his child.

Looking at the dome now, there was no moment of awe. The feeling of triumph he expected was missing. He felt only longing.

He turned away and saw the dog running over the top of a sand dune towards him.

In his head he recalled the exodus broadcast from the Patron.

"The environment is equivalent in size to the small gypsum moon of Arius, plenty of space for couplets to spread out and continue life like the suns had never burned out. We continue to defy the laws of entropy, forever building ourselves back up. We are a resilient race.

"There is much to look forward to in our new home. Look up and you will see an atmospheric dome specifically designed for our protection and, for regulating pressure, our meteorologists continue to monitor air composition and quality. In the case of undesirable changes in atmospheric conditions, the dome is designed to expel toxins through its membrane until the desired state is achieved once again. It's in a constant state of regulation. Our dome is strong enough to protect us from external forces, both natural and unnatural, and sensitive enough to predict even the slightest variations in our skies.

"On the ground, our landscape boasts fertile agricultural land to provide food, natural wildlife preserves, rolling plains and mountainous regions, lakes and rivers for us to enjoy, as well. We have developed a metropolis that emulates the civilized sectors to which we have become accustomed.

"We will dearly miss the beauty and elegance of the twin sisters on our skyline, but we will not be without the power they provided. After years of

~ ☾ ~

searching for alternate energy sources, our scientists have settled on a massive undertaking to import solar energy from a new star in the NGC 5866 galaxy. Think of it as a pipeline for solar power. Through their ingenuity the artificial environment will not be left in permanent midnight, but will be illuminated by solar panels that measure 100 meters square, stationed at regular intervals in the civilized colony. Plants and trees will continue to photosynthesize, creating the oxygen that we require. Weather patterns that are both our joy and our aggravation will continue to surprise us, with the exception of the unstable fronts that our meteorologists have now restricted.

"Friends, life in the artificial environment will be better than any civilization has experienced before. We will have our security, we will have our lifeblood, and we will have our freedom. We will have all the pleasures without the darkness.

"To those mutants who have successfully served the Policy, take heart, for you will be cared for and treated with equality. You will have access to all the environment has to offer. Fresh produce and meat will be shipped to stores in your community on a daily basis, originating from the very same farms and orchards enjoyed by the general population. Streams running directly through the heart of your sector will provide clean drinking water. You will have access to hunting grounds where you can seek out wild game and enjoy dinner killed with your very own hands. Fishing reservoirs will be in abundance. You and your couplet can live with more amenities than you have ever had before. Consider the artificial environment a place where you will live an enhanced version of the life you have known in the past. The two suns may have extinguished, but our new civilization will be stronger than ever before.

~ ☾ ~

"We live not in sickness, but in health ..."
Stanford knelt down to give the dog a scratch
behind the ears.
Sleep well, old boy ...
Sleep well ...

POWER OFF

~ ☾ ~

ACKNOWLEDGEMENTS

Gratitude goes out to my original editor, Leanne Sype, for believing in androids and more so for believing in the author. Thank you to Stephanie and Marlene at Crescent Moon for giving me a voice, and to my editor, Sheldon Reid, for making the story hum. To my boss at the newspaper all those years ago who gave an unproven young man his first chance to write for money; I promised I'd acknowledge you if I ever wrote a novel. I didn't forget, Mr. Werkman. And, of course, my deepest appreciation goes to all the special people who stood by me along the way. To Riki for putting up with my endless tinkering when this was only a short story in its embryonic stages; to Tara for her tireless efforts getting this thing off the ground, staying up late all those nights to hash it out – not to mention keeping me stocked with beer and cigars – I am forever grateful for the positive reinforcement. And to my parents, Pam and Lew, for their love and support – and occasional handout – I couldn't have done it without you. A million thanks to you all.

AUTHOR BIO

Chad Ganske was born in Red Deer, Alberta, Canada in 1976, relocating with his family to the small harbour town of Sidney, British Columbia, on Vancouver Island in the late eighties. After graduating from high school in 1994 he enrolled in the University of Victoria but left after one semester to enter the workforce. He slogged through a variety of entry level jobs before finally publishing his first novel, *Idyllic Avenue*. He presently resides in Victoria, British Columbia, where he spends a great deal of time alternating between states of elation and frustration while watching the Edmonton Oilers of the National Hockey League.

CPSIA information can be obtained at www.ICGtesting.com
Printed in the USA
LVOW06s0353150714

394290LV00001B/6/P